THE BUTTERSCOTCH PRINCE

THE
BUTTERSCOTCH
PRINCE
by Richard Hall

Boston • Alyson Publications, Inc.

Cover art by F. Ronald Fowler

Typeset and printed in the U.S.A

Second edition, first printing: August 1983

ISBN 0 932870 29 5

I. Cord

Now, sometimes, when I hear the new math teacher's voice floating down the hall from her classroom to mine, furious because her kids aren't paying attention, I can't believe she's right next door, separated by the same twenty yards of dirty linoleum that once separated me from Ellison. I never heard Ellison screaming at *his* ninth-graders, not till near the very end. He had that special quality that can turn thirty squirmers into a single learning machine.

When Ellison taught down the hall I never had to tap the door-stopper with my foot and swing it shut. Because his kids were pitched forward on their rubbery behinds, pencils gripped firmly, hot in pursuit of *x* the unknown. And loving it. You'd think *x* was the winning number in the state lottery or a prize thoroughbred at Aqueduct, the way they breathed. Ever hear thirty kids breathe while they use their heads eagerly, joyfully? They sound like the woodwind section playing the Forest Murmurs from *Siegfried*. Adenoidal ecstasy.

When you're a teacher you wait and hope for that. Forest Murmur time today — beautiful. That's your reward. The magic. The rest is only a job in a zoo. Sometimes, when a week or two go by and no Forest Murmurs, you start to wonder what drove you into exile among the Little People. What wrong turning? Are you atoning for wrong-doing in a previous life? Suffering from clogged veins or riboflavin deficiency? But don't get me wrong. I can't imagine doing any other kind of work. Most of the time.

But now, sometimes, when I hear the roars of Ginger Lucas down the hall and know she's standing in front of thirty flat blank faces, it seems only a bad dream. I even switch channels and pretend she isn't there. I view the bent heads in

7

my own class as we read about Tom Sawyer and Holden Caulfield and tell myself I'll meet Ellison in the faculty room for a smoke in a few minutes. And he'll punch me in the upper arm in that hostile-friendly way of his and his eyes will be soft with wariness and humor, two wet sherry-eyes at the bottom of the glass, and we'll trade a look that says everything.

Says, *Dig*, Mr. Rivkin the principal missed his prostate massage this morning because Luella, the school nurse, found the forefinger in her rubber glove all worn away. *Dig*, we're gonna buy old Horatio Hess, the French teacher, a Petite Larousse so he'll get his vocabulary over two thousand words. *Dig*, there's a new secretary named Awilda in the front office and we're gonna turn up wearing T-shirts that say *Puerto Rico Me Encanta*. *Dig*, buncha kids want to build a kite at lunchtime, a super-kite, let's give them a hand.

But none of that is going to happen now. When we drop Tom Sawyer and the kids look up and the Forest Murmurs fade (if they ever started) and Jesus Gongora jumps up with his right hand nailed to his crotch, I'm going to stay in my seat. I won't trundle downstairs to the faculty room. I'll lock my door for five minutes and sneak a smoke here. I can't take the vacancy there. The air is bent to his shape still, but where he should be, one eye squinty in an aureole of smoke, is emptiness. Ellison Greer, who used to complain about the view from his apartment on 22nd Street, now has the finest view in three states, a thousand-dollar-a-month condominium-type view from New Jersey, where the morning sun hits the glittering peaks of Manhattan and turns them into illustrations for the heavenly city. He's in the Elysian Fields Cemetery, Section 35, Plot B. The all-black section. With a puncture wound through his grieving heart.

Maybe I should introduce myself. Cordell McGreevy. That's one of the advantages of parenthood — one of the few, I guess. You get to name your creation. I was born 31 years ago, named for Cordell Hull, who was racing around signing peace treaties when my father was young. He was very impressed. Frankly, I've always felt kind of dated, like bread that says Good Until September 25th. Nobody knows Cordell Hull any more.

I grew up in Troy, New York, which is a nice place to be from. The best thing I can say about it is that if they chopped it off and moved it to a warmer clime I might like to go back. But since my father died and my mother moved to California, I can find no reason to return. I only had one friend there, the quietest boy in my class, who raised praying mantises professionally starting at the age of ten. He put curtain rings around their middles and tied them to the back fence with sewing thread, but I have a sneaky feeling he's tied up somewhere now with a curtain ring around his own middle.

I guess I had a standard American upbringing — everything rosy on the outside but inside a real House of Atreus, everybody full of pent-up wrath and plans for revenge. My sister and I have barely spoken to each other for ten years. Our last quarrel was over the division of spoils when my father died and my mother broke up housekeeping. Geri and I had a vicious fight over a book — an Oz book which we both loved — but it was one of those quarrels which is not really about the matter at hand. It was an ancient wrong with underground runners that went back and back, down and down, like oak roots under the front porch. Back to who got to sleep in Mom's bed. Who got to kiss Daddy first. Who got to ride in the front seat. God knows.

But as we stood in the upstairs hallway, snatching the Oz book from each other's hands, there was one moment when our eyes met and we both knew, deeply and truly, that we would never forgive or forget. That at the age of sixty, seventy, on our deathbeds, we would still be competing, still trying to push the other aside ("Me first, me first!"), still taking out old injustices and polishing them to a fine black glow (The Annual Awards Dinner for Grievances — this year's prize goes to Cord for his standout performance in *I Remember Mama*). And something in me went cold — a flame perishing — and I let her have the book. We have been cool ever since.

That story reflects no credit on me. I won't waste pages trying to justify myself, tracing our sibling rivalry to the same pounding hungers that exist in every family. It doesn't really matter, does it? I mean, all we've got is *now*.

One other story from the past — the last one, I promise — and one I like better. Not that it's any more flattering.

I studied piano as a kid, mostly under my mother's prodding. The worst part was the annual recital given by the students of my teacher, Miss diFlorenzo. This recital was a very classy affair at the Trojan Acres Club with the girl students (and the students were mostly girls, believe me) in evening dresses and the boy students (all three of us) in pre-tied bow ties. The recital was organized so that the most advanced students played last and one year — believe it or not — I was the most advanced. The last of the last.

9

Picture it. A six-foot grand on a dais (I used an upright at home). Acres of relatives out front, beaming with pleasure that their ordeal was almost over and the bar within easy reach. Miss diFlorenzo almost buried in a gardenia corsage she had sent herself. And yours truly, approaching the keyboard with the terrifying conviction that he couldn't play unless he went to the bathroom first and dropped a load.

The Chopin Funeral March, my scheduled offering, had gone clean out of my mind. Luckily, my fingers still remembered and I sat in remote bemusement watching them scuttle over the keys like mottled crabs, picking out sounds that seemed vaguely familiar. But all good things have to end and when the *da capo* came around, my fingers ran out of gas. So, after rippling off a handsome broken chord in the diminished, I spun around to the audience and said, "That is where Chopin died, ladies and gentlemen. The piece was finished by his star pupil, Ludwig van Beethoven, as you all know. But I'm sure you want me to end the piece here, where Chopin did, out of respect." Cool as ice, not a quaver in my voice. Naturally there was great applause — mostly because now they could hug their kids and head for the bar. But the pay-off came when Miss diFlorenzo rushed up and kissed me, her corsage going like sixty, and said in her birdy voice, "He did what Paderewski used to do. He always stopped there too. And he was a personal friend of the composer."

I tell this story not to show how weak is the hold of the average citizen on nineteenth century chronology, but to make another, sadder point — how easy it has always been for me to lie. Sometimes I think I was born with a tape running in my head, the Lie for Today. When faced with any difficulty, the tape starts and I get this homing feeling, the relief of knowing I'm back in the land of lies, all snuggled in and comfy, where no one can reach or harm me.

Even now, when my life is so different, I sometimes get the old urge and it takes a firm hold on the tape to keep it from rewinding and starting over. In my heyday I lied for no reason at all, just to keep in practice, or to tell my hearer something that could be believed more easily, wtihout an explanation. And that's why I've always made my friends people of integrity, those who make the rare stubborn stands of this world. No one else interests me. That was true even when I was a kid, which explains why Miss diFlorenzo found herself minus a star pupil after the recital.

How I got from Troy to teaching in P.S. 9 in Manhattan is

a long boring story, mostly about sitting in classrooms and taking notes and regurgitating the notes on exam forms, plus a few years of therapy to help me bridge the gap between the glorious bullshit of college and the brutality of the West Side. That's one way of putting it. Actually, two years with Dr. Ash were spent learning how to be a fag.

I put it that way because things are better now and I can joke about it. That is, I can be self-deprecating in a mildly humorous way, which Dr. Ash always said is a sign of "maturity" — a word, I've always believed, that should be applied to bonds and not people. But learning How T.B.A.F. was not as easy as it sounds.

I know, these days, it's supposed to be a smooth transition from a world that hates you to a world that loves you, a smooth boogie from an old life to a new. Read the pride manuals, go to a few rap sessions, turn out for some zaps, march in the June parade, and whammo! — there's nothing to be afraid of. You're automatically rid of the scorn ("Hey, man, you throw that ball like a girl!") and the fear ("You didn't get a hard-on when you danced with Cindy, whazza matter with ya?"). Well, it didn't work out that way for me.

In fact, there were some very heavy times, when I figured I wasn't going to make it. I had to develop a whole new cell structure that could handle it — a Cordell McGreevy clone that could cope with cocksucking, as it were. It wasn't easy. In fact, I suspect that even Dr. Ash, a balding model of subdued optimism nailed to a black Barcalounger, occasionally had his doubts.

Like the week I couldn't stop talking, after overhearing two men my own age, in the ad agency where I worked as a copywriter, discuss the fact that I was queer. I was visiting a colleague in his topless cubicle when my name sounded over the glass bricks — my name followed by a few estimates of my sex habits. I stumbled out, ears roaring, back to my own cubicle. That afternoon a silver thread of sound started pouring from my mouth. It didn't stop for fourteen hours a day for seven days. I talked to every human being who crossed my path. When you figure I was riding the buses and roaming the streets, that adds up to a lot of people. Most of them, and it's a credit to New York, were courteous, perhaps realizing I was *in extremis* but harmless. I talked about everything and nothing — a blind rush of chatter that kept the lid on the hysteria. I don't want to get clinical, because this story is about Ellison Greer and others, but as I analyzed it later, with Dr. Ash's help, my talking enabled me to hold on. It was the glue that held the shreds and tatters of my ego together. The wind in the sails of my self. I talk therefore I am. As simple as that.

I met Ellison Greer not long after the talkathon. I was still shaky but at least I'd hung up my harp. I'll never forget the shock of seeing him. Not because he was handsome, although he was. No. Because Ellison Greer, except for his smaller size and the amount of melanin in his skin, could have been my twin. If I describe him you can see us both. Just reduce his dimensions by ten percent.

Broad forehead, a blade nose, a chin that won the west. Brown eyes, shading up to amber in a certain light. His best feature is hard to describe and I spotted it instantly. I'd call it natural grace, the unbought kind. He hung well, light and bouncy, ballbearings under his feet. Coat-hanger shoulders, snake hips and an ass that bobbed up like two apples in a basin. An aristocrat in a shadowed skin. A butterscotch prince.

I met Ellison in the lobby of the Lyric Theater, and I don't mean an opera house. It was on East 14th Street, in the heart of mango land, San Juan North. The Lyric, for those who haven't had the pleasure, is a browsing pasture for dedicated trophy hunters, sword swallowers. On screen was hard-core pornography, dicks like barbers' poles, vaginas deep as the San Andreas Fault. You wouldn't believe how dull fucking can be until you sit through two hours of it. After a while you think you're in an auto body shop.

Why did I go? A good question. I can give you the usual reasons — loneliness, boredom, sexual dementia, etc. But none of them is exactly right. What drove me to the Lyric was — to quote one of Dr. Ash's more sententious remarks — my "identity crisis." It was a place in which to find the mantle of a self and wrap it around me. Those hungry Hildas roving the aisles, those human suction machines, gave me a sense of myself. Cord McGreevy as a member of a group. Some group. A far-fetched psychiatric theory, obviously, but you'd be surprised how well it tested out. Because when I was dissatisfied or annoyed, when I'd told one lie too many and lost what little sense of myself I had, the need to hit the Lyric would come down on me like the vengeance of the Lord and I would find myself transported to the goblin palace with the white marquee that said Adult Films Only.

Cleopatra didn't ride her barge with greater glee than I did the crosstown bus. Just buying the ticket from the lady with polyester hair was a high. Handing it to the ticket man, who was once a star in the Yiddish theater around the corner, buoyed me up even more. And when I hit the interior, fruity with the groinsmell of a hundred desperate men, I could feel every muscle go loose with excitement. Gliding around that black cavern was as soothing as a lobotomy. Up and down I went, noiseless, my steps cushioned by the carpet, down to the can, out to the alleys on either side, past rows of men, eyes to the screen, caught up in those vast meaningless couplings. As I moved around I could feel my edges soften, the boundary that separated me from life begin to blur.

The strangest thing at the Lyric calmed me the most — the utter silence. No one spoke. I doubt that fifty live sentences have been spoken in that place since it went porno. Meeting, touching, climaxing — all without a word. As if a new convention of language had been minted, the language of gliding feet and bent head, of sudden gasp and sodden sigh. I felt as if I were lapped in the womb of some prehistoric sea, before creatures hit dry land and cried.

I saw Ellison in the outer lobby, at the foot of the stairs to the balcony. Our eyes clicked at the same moment. Look-alikes. Brothers under the skin. The phrase hit me like a blow. He was a tawny gold, a lovely Gauguin gold. He had one foot on the stairs but he turned around and came toward me with the mocking smile I got to know so well, a smile full of things like, "Is this meat market really you?" Or, "I won't tell your mama if you won't tell mine."

Actually, he came up to me and said, "I wanta talk to you." I was very surprised. I mean, no one had ever said a word to me in that place, much less indicated interest in sustained conversation. My first reaction was negative. I wanted out. I glanced at the curtained doors leading inside but he read my mind. "Uh-uh," he shook his head sweetly and jerked his thumb toward the exit. "Out." And then he snapped his fingers. A soft sound, hardly audible, almost too faint for any ears but his. *Snap!* How many thousands of times I was to hear those gold castanets going off!

With a mastery that permitted no protest, he conducted me to the street. Ellison never got flapped, which is another way of saying his surfaces were polished as smoked glass. Underneath, of course, there's another tale to tell, a tale leading to Section 35, Plot B. But that first night I didn't glimpse anything but self-control and integrity. The kind I couldn't resist.

We sat over coffee for a long time, not really saying much except for the required gripes about living in New York. I remember his first contribution to that — "New York is the only place where you go to bed with clean fingernails and wake up with an inch of crud."

It was strange looking at him. The white-tiled glare of the shop made me squint after the dark theater but I noticed details. His hands were squarish, like mine, with long knobby fingers. His eyebrows were straight and narrow — pencil slashes, over deep sockets. His hair was a coarse wiggy fiber mounded high. His teeth were piano keys, a C-major smile.

Ellison was born in Elizabeth, New Jersey, went to Jefferson High there, then to North Bergen State, staying on for an advanced degree in education. He always planned to be a math teacher. Only once did he waver, when he went to work for Chase Manhattan right after graduation, having received from a recruiter an offer too good to turn down. But it soured quickly. "I was window dressing," he said. "I got my picture in the house organ seven times in twelve months. The day I found myself looking at my face in a full-page ad in the *Times* I figured it was time to quit. I was turning into an illustrated man."

I listened to that story but my senses, my blood and nerves, were soaking up a different line. I was trembling with that message, scourged with its possibilities. I had been a single person, a unit of aloneness, all my life. Was now, tonight, with this man who resembled me so strangely, the beginning of something new? But even as I wondered this, in some portion of my mind where no lies are possible I knew that nothing was going to happen. Nothing. Almost from the moment we met, Ellison Greer and I were ex-lovers.

Finally he smiled his C-major smile and said, "Your place or mine?"

"Yours." I needed that last freedom, the freedom to get up and walk out. He reached for the check and off we went.

Ellison lived on the West Side, just a subway hop from me. I was on Morton Street in the Village in an over-priced closet; he was on West 22nd Street, a block with good renovated brownstones. He was proud of the block. "I know most all the people around here," he said, exaggerating hopelessly.

His apartment was a mix of good things and junk — cheap lacquered chairs and a fine Byobu screen, a battered Parsons

14

table and some nice prints by Paul Signac. The main feature was the record and tape collection. The stereo dominated one wall. Ellison liked everything, apparently — Bessie Smith, Charles Trenet, Arthur Schnabel, Ravi Shankar, Bob Marley, Elisabeth Schwarzkopf. Of course there weren't many books. That didn't surprise me. Math teachers are allergic to the printed word. They usually can't spell.

I sat on the couch and watched him put on a Rosa Ponselle record. He flipped me the record jacket and went to the kitchen for beers. The *Casta diva*, ice sculpture by Bellini, floated from four speakers. I sat back and tried not to think.

He came back with the beers and dropped onto the couch beside me. I thought he'd burn a hole in the air with his body heat. I could smell it — an odor of singed fabric and Tabac.

After a few sips he put down his beer, leaned over and kissed me. His lips were little suction cups. Then he pulled back and searched my face. "Nice," he murmured without much conviction.

I put my hand next to his. They were almost the same size. Only the one difference.

"One chocolate, one vanilla," he said.

"More butterscotch I'd say."

He smiled at that. "I'm butterscotch all over," he said. "You want to see?"

He must have read the uneasiness in my eyes, because he changed the subject. We talked about music for a while. I told him about my piano career and Miss diFlorenzo.

"Man," he commented, "when I was a kid, I never had to do anything, eat anything I didn't like. You got any talent?"

"No."

He swung his head slowly from side to side. "A social worker get holda you she'd have you in a foster-home before you could say Johann Sebastian Bach."

He leaned back, his face frozen with soundless laughter. I leaned over and kissed him. When I finished he looked at me carefully. "I have the feeling you got... shall we say, some doubts."

"How can you tell that?"

"From the way you kiss. Like you're following the book of instructions."

Stung, I leaned over and attacked his mouth with my own. He let me finish, then sighed. "You're just making it worse. Time to flip Miss Ponselle. Excuse me."

He got up and I watched him bounce across the room.

When he turned his profile I felt a tiny explosion inside me. He must have read my mind because he said, "You and I, we might be cousins, you think of that?"

"Yes, I have."

"All the states were slave-holding once. Maybe your great-great raped my great-great. Right around New York."

I shrugged. "What's the difference?"

He shrugged too, coming back. "No difference." He paused and studied me. "You ever had a lover?" When I didn't answer he raised his eyebrows. "Just hit and run."

It was coming, I thought. The pitch for permanence. As before, in the coffee-shop, a warm hope went throught me, followed by its opposite. I could only lie to myself for about a minute.

"Me, I'm in the market for something steady," he went on. "I dunno why I'm saying that. Last guy I told that to got so nervous he cut his lip on the beer can. On his way out." His eyes held mine for a long moment. "Door's open," he said.

"To tell you the truth, I'm more interested in a friend than a lover."

He shook his head. "You get yourself a lover, anything over that, like friendship, is velvet."

I shook my head and he continued. "What makes you think you and me, we can be friends?" When I didn't reply he said, "The place to make friends is in the sack. That's where your body does the talkin'. The rest is mostly bullshit."

He looked at me, trying to read me, and something flickered in his eyes — hope maybe, or the first tremor of it. I couldn't be sure because the beautiful mocking smile was back in place almost at once.

"Funny," he said, "I get the feeling we're applying for a divorce before we even get married."

I laughed. "Where's the wedding bed?" It was time to end this particular conversation.

His body was what I expected — smooth curving chest, taut arms, round flat nipples pasted on like decals. His pubic hair was bronze; he had my square knees. He kept his eyes on my face while we undressed, but finally looked down.

"I see another difference," he said.

"Yeah."

"The rabbi cut me and he left you alone."

"Don't hold it against me."

"Gonna hold it against you all night if I want."

He crossed the space between us, moving sinuously

through the reddened air of the bedroom, and took my face between his hands. His tongue flickered in and out of my mouth, over my eyelids and cheeks.

"This is gonna be real good," he said.

We lay down together and he began to explore my body with gentle precision. Finding the buttons, avoiding the circuit breakers. Talking to my nerves, a tender sustained conversation with my neural pathways that made them jerk into life. But midway through, don't ask me why, something happened. An intrusion, a refusal, a fear jarred loose from the past. I don't know. Maybe we'd already started on the road to brotherhood and it was too late for raw sex — two bodies smacking like flounders in the bottom of the pail. We did all the required things, helping each other, but the bed didn't fly us to the moon. The orgasm, when it came was. . . well, earthbound. He took my seed in his mouth — working me carefully, selflessly — while manipulating himself. I didn't hear or see him climax. When he flopped down, sighing, I knew he was disappointed. He had hoped for more. I was disappointed too, of course, but in another way I was glad it hadn't worked out differently. I knew the road from here on. Back to my over-priced closet on Morton Street, back to the bars and baths and the Lyric. The other road would have been unmarked. Terrifying.

"See," I murmured, tracing the gully down the center of his chest, "we don't really fly together."

"You never let go."

I felt a twinge of guilt. "I do sometimes."

"With who? Somebody rapes you?"

He hissed out his breath and turned away. I waited. Finally I said, "You want me to go?"

He answered in a small voice, still turned away. "No."

You want me to spend the night?"

His voice squeezed out, a thin ribbon of sound. "You too stupid to go out this time of night." He turned back toward me and laid one arm across my chest. Looking in his eyes, two warm berries on the pillow beside me, I felt something in me soften, something that had been balled into a hard knot all evening. I kissed him on his eyes with a low contented sound. He laughed out loud and pressed his body into mine, holding me so that we merged into a tangle of limbs. When he released me his irises were huge. "I hope you like fried chicken," he said.

We smoked and talked. I told him about Dr. Ash, who

was always spouting gay liberation but hadn't really been able to liberate me. Funny, talking about him that night was like punctuating him. Putting an end to that period of my life.

Ellison told me about his marriage. He talked about it lying on his back, blowing smoke rings through the reddish air. They had met while he was working on his M.A. "I was living with her off-campus. She was getting a graduate degree too. Fine arts, art history. She was one bright chick. Taught me. . ." he nodded toward the living room, ". . .all about music. Lots of things. We were goin' along, both of us workin' hard — I had a night job at a drive-in bank just off the Turnpike. And then I decided. . ." I heard the hesitation in his voice, ". . .maybe she could straighten me out. Like if I married her. Keep me from messin' around here and there. You know?"

He turned toward me. I nodded.

"She was real sensitive. And tough at the same time. I didn't have to spell things out for her. We dug each other." He paused, dragged on his cigarette. "Her parents were real nice cats. Lived up in New England." He crinkled his eyes. "Abolitionists from way back. They figured we were good for each other."

"How long were you married?"

He took his time replying. "About two years. Till after we graduated. She wanted to go off to California to look for a teaching job. Me, I wanted to stay here. That wasn't the real reason, though. The real reason was — we weren't making it too good in the sack any more. My old bad habits." He sighed, but it sounded more like a groan. "No more marriage for me."

"How did she take that?"

"Not too good. Kinda bad, in fact." His voice became dreamy. I waited, but the pause lengthened.

At last I said, "What is it you really want?"

He leaned up on one elbow, suddenly harsh. "I don't want nothin' except learnin' those kids about the icy beauty of numbers. And on Friday I want to go to the Lyric The-aytur and suck cock in the doorway to the men's room." A tearing sound came form his throat. "And after that I want to come home and listen to good music."

He twisted away from me but I reached for him, pulling him back, elongating my legs next to his so that the bones clicked. And I knew that this was a significant moment, maybe the most significant we would ever have, when everything would go one way or another. But this wasn't a movie

18

and I wasn't Burt Reynolds. I was Cord McGreevy with the furies slamming around in my guts, and when Ellison suddenly flooded into life, his need and desire overwhelming me, I couldn't match him. Couldn't find it. Something in me just. . . wouldn't. And when he found himself unaccompanied, he slid away from me, and I felt our aloneness in that bed more deeply than anything I can remember. For a full minute we lay on our sides, looking into each other's eyes. In his I read defeat. Pity. Anger, maybe, then slowly resignation. I guess he saw the panic in mine, or heard the whirring noise. because at last he cradled me in his arms and whispered, "Hush up, hush up." Although I spent the night in his arms, I never made love with Ellison again. And I never stopped loving him.

II. Ellison

Then the good years started. Relatively speaking. What can I say about Ellison in that time? First, I ate a lot of fried chicken. Plus homemade bread and chess pie and watermelon pickles brought back from trips to his mother in Elizabeth. I heard a lot of music I liked and just as much I didn't. Gradually we settled into homey routines — shopping, entertaining, sleeping over.

Of course, we had our ups and downs. Sometimes I felt hemmed in by his mothering, his advice. He had unkind names for me too — Mr. Fly-by-Night, Miss Laid, and after I joined a gym, Old Lats and Pecs. Sometimes he came on to me, especially if he'd been drinking or smoking, but he was easy to refuse. Only once, high on some dynamite weed, did he get nasty. After a lecture on chastity he snarled, "I heard of the zipless fuck but you're somethin' else — you're the fuckless zip."

But under our differences there was. . . symbiosis. Together, it seemed to me, we made one person. I don't know how much our physical resemblance contributed to that. It was always there, the Gemini thing. Jared Green called us the Paper Dolls ("Yeah," Ellison said to that, "the same scissors but different paper.") Sometimes, too, I wondered if there was only gay narcissism involved, self-love.

Whatever the reason for it, our closeness kept us from forming household arrangements with anyone else. There were pickups, of course. We'd talk about each other's latest, and once or twice swapped them. But if it went beyond the one-night stage, fuck and goodbye, there was tension.

I remember a charming Frenchman, my own age, who walked into my cubicle at the baths, sat down and started to

20

talk. His name was Guy Marceau, he loved America after three days, and why didn't anybody make conversation in this place? I started on one of my half-baked theories about the strong silent type as the American erotic ideal — something observed in a thousand cowboy movies — and before you knew it, we were running a heavy discussion of French vs. American iconography. I mean, in the baths, while all around us the heavy sounds of male orgasm were rising and falling, heightened occasionally by the slap of a belt on a bare buttock. And when we got finished, believe it or not, we moved into marvelous sex. He had a tight little body, with clear, almost translucent skin on which dark hair fizzed up here and there. We ended up making as much noise as everybody else.

I had dinner with him a few nights later — how could I refuse his request for my phone? — and found him delightful out of bed too. I liked the way he used his knife and fork, critiqued the Gallo, loved New York. He'd been sent over by a French winery to work in their local office — for which he'd studied English for six months. He shrugged a lot.

Ellison got wind of Guy after my third date — I used "we" at the wrong time and had to fill him in. I guess he heard something new in my voice because he got very quiet, so quiet I could almost hear his pulse. At last he said, "Sounds like you got yourself a soul-mate." His eyes were puddles of pain and his chest — the chest I knew so well — heaved briefly. And the next instant I knew I couldn't be disloyal to Ellison, couldn't throw over our friendship, our easy habits — not for a new trick. Ellison read every sequence of my thought, though I didn't say a word, and the next few times Guy called I made excuses. Finally I heard no more from him. Ellison and I went out for a gala dinner the following weekend, to celebrate the reforging of our bond. I was a bit resentful — I felt I had been manipulated — but under the resentment, I knew that I really preferred this arrangement. I was safe with Ellison.

He talked me out of my job in the ad agency. It wasn't hard to do. After they moved me to the GM account and I came up with a slogan the client loved ("Something to believe in"), I got depressed. Ellison roared when I told him I was socko in Detroit. "Something to believe in — a Chevrolet? What kind of bullshit is that? Where's your self-respect?"

Three weeks later I gave notice.

Ellison had offered to pay my expenses while I went for an M.A. but I borrowed some money from my mother, ate dried lima beans three nights a week and cut out restaurant meals, new clothes and sex places. I listened to those professors mouth platitudes about pedagogy, sensing all the time, without ever having set foot in a classroom, that the problems I would face would have no connection to their theories. They would connect through my hair and fiber and bone to what Dr. Ash used to call, lovingly, my identity.

I graduated before tough times brought on the hiring freeze. Ellison, through some fancy string-pulling on Livingston Street, got me through the interviews, sample teaching sessions and general inspection. I was even lucky enough to skip the substitute route, again thanks to Ellison's contacts with what he called the Black Hand — the School-Based Support Team at the Regional Co-ordinator's Office. I wound up in the same P.S. 9 where he worked — a stucco and brick monstrosity in the West Eighties.

At first I thought teaching would kill me. But slowly, without realizing it, it shaped and toughened and refined me. I became the sum of the scolding and threatening and loving that went on in the classroom. I found — or invented — myself. After four years the young man who sat on Dr. Ash's couch whimpering about Mommy and Daddy was laid to rest in the ashes of his own traumas.

I don't want to sentimentalize teaching. It was a three-tiered thing of frustration, agony and joy. I'm not sure I could have survived without Ellison down the hall, ripe with projects that would bring Forest Murmur sounds out of the kids. Like the day we found the corpse in the basement supply room.

Ellison and I had finished lunch early and gone down looking for graph paper. The room was unlocked, which was unusual, since half the staff in that school would strip the storeroom of everything, given the chance. Behind one of the cartons of new books we found a sneakered foot. It belonged to Preston Ware, who had dropped out the year before and was now dealing in front of the candy store across the street — a boy caught fatally in the trade he plied, o.d.'d with his own rotten stuff.

Ellison and I gazed at him for a long minute, hardly breathing. Then he said, "Why don't we bring the kids down here this afternoon?" I could hardly believe my ears. "You kidding?" "No. The lesson for the day is right here. Cord, this is what we gotta teach 'em. This." He tapped his toe against Preston's foot and I knew he was right, just as I knew we'd catch hell when Rivkin heard about it.

So, instead of reporting it, we brought our students to the basement in small groups, where they stood around in breathless silence — death, I suppose, is the only force mighty enough to still the tongues of adolescence — staring at the stiff remains of Preston Ware, his rolled-up eyes staring out of his face like pig-pong balls. His death reached the kids because it was death in person, not death on the tube or half a planet away, and because most of them knew more about drugs in the ninth grade than I would know at any age. I hope it made a lasting impression on them (you never know) because, sure enough, Rivkin almost fired us. I mined that episode for a week of compositions and even worked up a mock TV show featuring the life and times of Preston Ware. Perhaps it was his greatest — and only — contribution to his community.

We traveled together in the summer. One year we did a bike tour of the Lake District in England. When I walked into the Wordsworth cottage with Ellison or lay on a slope above Tintern Abbey with him, I thought earth had nothing to show more fair. He even tolerated my reading the poet's works aloud, in my corny English-teacher way, with his mocking smile partially suppressed.

Another summer we toured the Adriatic via a tacky little Yugoslav steamer called the Jadran, in whose bar the plum slivovitz was dirt cheap. I suppose we seemed an odd couple to the other passengers — two males, strangely twinned, sharing a cabin. No doubt they thought we were lovers, and in most ways they would have been right. But in actual fact our strangeness lay in our distance, not our camaraderie — though that would have been hard to explain to a European.

Not that we were virginal. Besides the gay pick-ups, we teamed up once with two German girls — big Brunnhilde types who worked as secretaries in Frankfurt. We met them at the terrace bar of a hotel in Dubrovnik and after quite a bit to drink paired off with them. I went to Trude's room; Ellison took Lise to ours. At first I was terribly intimidated by her breasts — they seemed to deform her firm, almost muscular body — and I thought I couldn't do anything. But then, in a sudden flip-flop that might have been due to the booze, I was stunned by their beauty, thrilled by their doughy pliability. Fron time to time Trude giggled and thought up new things to do. She must have been pleased when it was over because she invited me to Frankfurt, urging me to call her collect.

Afterward, Ellison ordered a bottle of spumante to celebrate the end of that particular virginity for me. We drank until we passed out in our room and the gauzy Adriatic fog drifted in to wake us with its chill.

Now, looking back, I see that Ellison had begun to change during that summer in Yugoslavia — our next to last abroad. In ways easy to overlook. Little things made him angry — a bellboy who delayed bringing up our luggage in Zagreb, a street boy who tagged after us in Split, a desk clerk who made a mistake with the bill in Pula. Several times I had to pull him away, snarling, and make him sit in a café to get control of himself.

He began to change physically, though I was the last to see it. But other friends noticed that he had gotten thinner, his cheekbones sharpening, his frame getting more wiry.

After we got home in August, his older brother died of lung cancer. His mother, a crisp woman of 74, was greatly affected. Her mind seemed to vary between light and darkness; she had trouble finishing sentences. Ellison had to go to Elizabeth on weekends to cook a whole week's meals for her. She refused to move out of her house.

One Sunday evening, seeing him after he came back to the city, I had the impression that something in him was drying out. The juices were not flowing. His brother's death, his mother's illness, seemed to be accelerating whatever process had begun in Europe. The old tart sweetness that I knew so well seemed to be changing into something else, something chemically quite different. I kept asking him stupid things, like "What's the matter?" "What's going on?" But these only made him turn away, pour himself a drink, curse.

My misgivings were confirmed when I went in his classroom one day in October to borrow a blackboard eraser. He was in a fury, his body shaking. The students were cowering in their seats. Several were crying. Whatever had set him off — and it might have been something justifiable — his reaction was too much. I'd never walked into that classroom before and found something ugly.

I began to see less of him. One evening a week instead of three or four. Less given, less taken. I almost never went up to spend the night. Of course, his mother's illness was partly the reason. Most weekends he wasn't in town. But even at school, at lunch-time, I saw him less. He seemed to prefer the company of Liz Garrity, a new teacher this term, plump and blonde and full of wild whooping laughter. I could see she had a lech for Ellison — see it from the way her hands rested on his arm across the cafeteria table, the way she brought him coffee in the faculty room. Well, she wasn't the first. A lot of women had made passes at Ellison, to no avail. I doubted that Liz Garrity would break through to make real contact.

Of course, it wasn't all anger and indifference. We had some good times during that last year, just like the old days. We took a bunch of kids to Coney Island, Liz Garrity asking if she could come along. It turned out that Ellison was scared of the Cyclone — really scared, something to do with a plane crash he'd once walked away from. When the kids found out, they gave him no peace. Just turned into twenty devils, determined to drag him on the damned rollercoaster. At last, with everybody pulling, including Liz, he walked through the turnstile. He was sweating when he got off, but his simple act of overcoming an old fear welded us into a triumphant phalanx for the rest of the afternoon. And there, with three or four kids hanging on each side of him, I saw the old Ellison. He even did his famous cigarette trick — the stub in one ear, smoke issuing from his mouth. Liz appreciated the change in him too, because instead of being bossy she subsided into a sweet motherliness, playing word-games with the kids, buying them corn-on-the-cob and cotton candy.

I hoped this excursion would turn Ellison back to his cheerful self, but it didn't. As the school year wore on, he remained distant, preoccupied. It was easy to believe he was avoiding me. Several times, when he told me he was too beat for even a quiet evening, I had to go up and ring his bell, unannounced. At those times I had the feeling he was merely tolerating me.

I was counting on the trip to Italy to bring us together again that last summer. Ellison had wanted to go to the hill towns for years, and this time we were going to make it — hotels booked, car reserved, the works. When he talked about it, some of the old sparkle came back. "Gonna go over there and find out if St. Francis was using some kind of see-ment to hold those birds on his shoulders." He even bought an Italian phrase book and spent his evenings taping questions and answers. When he played them for me, I broke up. He was hissing out a language never heard on land or sea.

At last the big day came. Hamilton Thorpe and Paul Ferrara were going to drive us out to Kennedy. They were a loving pair — Hamilton in his mid-forties, Paul ten years younger. They'd known Ellison long before I met him. They ran a shop and decorating service.

But the send-off went sour. We'd made plans to meet in

Spoleto, all four of us, for what remained of the famous festival. But as we neared the TWA terminal, all of us admiring that concrete eagle trying to soar, Ellison said, "Cord and I have decided not to go to Spoleto after all."

I was too surprised to react at first. I thought, for a moment, he was joking. But he wasn't. Hamilton, at the wheel, took it well. I looked in the rear-view mirror and saw he didn't even blink. "You two decide whatever you want," he said, "it's okay with us."

"You two!" I managed at last. "This is the first I heard of it!"

Paul said nothing, just creased his aquiline face into a nervous smile.

"What about tickets?" I turned to Ellison beside me in the back seat. "What about the hotel?"

He said nothing, but I knew the signs of anger held in check, a panther on a leash. "What the fuck is the matter with you?" I added, almost shouting.

He replied quietly, through clenched teeth. "You go on to Spoleto if you want. I don't dig being around all the hairdressers in Europe for a week."

"Are you telling me..."

And then his mask dropped. "I said you go alone!"

The goodbyes were strained. Hamilton and Paul saw us to the check-point, their kind remarks too emphatically polite. I was quietly furious. After they cleared our hand luggage, I started in again. "You've been rude as hell to your friends," I started.

He stopped dead in the hallway. "Don't bug me with this, Cord."

"You change your mind without consulting anybody and you expect me not to bug you?"

He took a deep breath then uttered a single word. "Please." Our eyes locked. In his I saw such deep confusion mixed with anger that I knew I would yield. There was something he wanted to work out alone. In silence. I foresaw a summer like the previous one — only worse. When we reached the loading area I flung myself into a plastic seat and opened a paperback. I didn't look up until they called our flight.

I was right about the summer. Most of the time I was with someone who had moved apart. It was like sitting in the snow and watching a strange city burn. Sometimes, in the long hours we spent in cafés, he would look up from the crossword puzzle in the *Trib* and I would catch a certain look in his eyes. As if he were trying to signal me, trying to flag me down on my parallel road and ask me to come aboard with him. But he only tried hard, with words, once. We had worked our way through the glowing browns and greens of Umbria and Tuscany and wound up in Venice. It was a cloudy afternoon, too cool for the Lido. We were having an ice at Florian's, looking out the window at the vast enclosed piazza that Napoleon called the drawing room of Europe. A tacky orchestra, under the arcade, was playing the Barcarolle, in case the tourists forgot where they were. Ellison closed his eyes briefly in pleasure at the sight and sound. When he opened them I found myself facing the old dry sweetness I knew so well.

"I guess I've been a little hard to be around," he said.

I looked at him carefully. "If I don't know what's bothering you there's nothing I can do to help."

"What's bothering me," he repeated. His eyebrows shot up and he spooned some zabaglione. "What's bothering me is... the high price of ass around here."

"Come on."

He sat motionless for a moment, his skin almost green in the shadow of the portico. His voice was light and remote when he spoke. "See, if I have to tell you it won't help. No way." I didn't answer and he went on. "Remember what I told you that first night? About body talk?" He looked at me hard and I felt myself flush. I dropped my eyes and he shifted his legs. "That wouldn't have made any difference either," he said, his voice more empty than before.

I forced myself to continue the subject. "I don't think you're telling the truth. If we had..."

"Do I look like I'm perishin' to get my hands on you?" His eyes were tender.

"No."

"You seen me goin' without these last few years?"

"No."

"Well then." He picked five lumps of sugar from the bowl on the table and dropped them on the table. Then he took out a sixth lump and held it up. "See this lump? He wants to get in with the others. Mix, be happy." He dropped the sixth lump on the table and jumbled them all together. "They want him in too. Come on in, they say. But this guy..." he picked out the sixth cube again, "...doesn't believe them. See, he thinks that deep down he's not like sugar at all. He's salt. Maybe he

27

looks like sugar, acts like sugar, even tastes like sugar. But down where his electrons are flyin' around his neutrons, he's salt." He looked up at me, measuring my face. "It's not you and me, Cord. It's sugar and salt." The lightness in his voice cracked on that, like a veneer left out in bad weather, and he snapped his fingers for the check. And the next night we met Vito.

We'd gone over to the Lido for dinner — there was a place there famous for its scampi — and when we chugged back across the Guidecca in that toy steamboat, watching the lights of Venice get bigger and brighter, all the discord of the past few weeks seemed to fade away. I felt myself unite with Ellison in the sight of that star-hung city, join with him in celebrating its peculiar magic. As we stood at the rail I rested my hand on his for a moment. I heard him exhale ever so slightly as we touched. Then he slid his hand away and glanced behind him. I thought I saw a shadow move against the pilothouse, but I wasn't sure — or didn't want to be sure.

But when we stepped across the half-rotted board that served as a gangplank, I became aware that someone was following us. Ellison glanced behind too frequently for me to ignore it. At last he stopped near the column in the piazzetta and waited. It was a thin, sallow boy of seventeen, with red-rimmed eyes and a bowsprit of a nose. He was dressed in a sagging nylon parka over a dirty gondolier's shirt. He seemed to cringe perpetually, as if expecting a blow. He spoke in a wheezy dialect without charm.

As Ellison made contact, I stood apart, trying to stem a rising tide of anger and self-righteousness. To use this creature was a form of scavenging. His history was all too plain — a wasted spirit, the detritus of a corrupt society — even though what had made him so was clearly no fault of his own. But even while these thoughts ravaged me, I knew I had no right to them. I had abdicated that right years ago. I had made a narrow bed and I would have to lie in it.

I strolled up and down the Riva degli Schiavone while Ellison took the boy back to the hotel. I didn't want this last night in Venice to be ruined. God knows how long before I would see the old stones again. But the delight had disappeared. Even standing in the spot where Byron, in one of his letters, wrote of being serviced by a young man dressed as a woman during Carnival brought on no tingle of pleasure. Literary scandal seemed pointless and stale.

I waited a suitable length of time, then returned to the

hotel. Ellison was lying on his back smoking. He didn't turn his head when I walked in. After a while, when I had turned off the light and beaten the bolster into some semblance of a pillow, he remarked casually that Vito — that was the boy's name — would travel to Rome with us tomorrow. I didn't answer, letting my disapproval wash around the room in heavy waves.

But Vito turned up the next morning, still wearing the yellow parka over the dirty gondolier's shirt. He had no other personal belongings. He rode in the back seat of the car, crying for us to stop every twenty kilometers so he could buy something to eat or go to the toilet. We spent one night in Florence, then made it to Rome the following evening.

We were staying at the Nazionale, just below the Spanish Steps, a second-class hotel whose staff found nothing unusual about our menage, I'm sure. But the boy's presence was galling to me. His smell, his eating habits, his possession of Ellison — everything irritated me. Finally, unable to stand the stench of his only shirt I insisted that Ellison buy him a new one. As a special concession I washed the old one, noting a kidney-shaped stain that wouldn't come out. It had probably been there since the time of the Doges.

Finally, the third night I announced I couldn't take another evening together. They were doing *Norma* in the Forum — I'd catch it alone. But I came back earlier than expected. The performance had been rotten. I didn't want to hear those two sopranos massacre one more duet. As it turned out, even walking got me to the hotel too early. I found a strange scene. Vito, naked except for his flesh-colored G-string, was huddled in a corner, whimpering, his hands in front of him. Ellison was standing in the center of the room, his bare chest heaving, his eyes ablaze. The rest of the room was a mess — the mattress sloping, the sheets twisted on the floor. Vito ran toward me, seizing my hand and pressing it to his face. Ellison cursed and went in the bathroom. I told Vito to dress in his new clothes and pushed him out the door with all the cash I had, which was considerable. He rolled the wad of lire in his earthen hands and looked suddenly content. Ellison stayed in the bathroom for half an hour and his face, when he came out, told me not to ask questions. Only now, after his death, can I guess what happened.

A slow frustration settled into our bones for the remainder of the trip. Several times I considered cancelling out and getting the next plane home. But a kind of dogged stubbornness took over and we went on with our itinerary — down to Naples, over to Capri — like soldiers on campaign. Ellison spent most of his days and nights roaming the streets alone, his eyes fastened on the locals. After we'd been on Capri a week he suddenly announced he wanted to go back to Rome, alone, for a few days. It was the last straw. I let him go, wondering if he had a way to contact Vito. When I returned we spent a day in almost total silence then flew home, a week early. There was no point in pretending any more. Our relationship was like dead coral — the living part of it had stopped growing. We were lost in a sea of misunderstanding.

The phone call came on the Sunday of Labor Day Weekend, September third. We'd been back a week. It was from his landlady, Mary Battaglia. She lived on the parlor floor of the brownstone on 22nd Street, a big handsome woman with a vivid wardrobe.

"Cord? This is Mary Battaglia." It was II a.m. and her voice was hushed with shock. A cold sweat formed in the small of my back. "The police are here. Something's happened."

She stopped, unable to go on, and I had to repeat her name several times. At last she whispered, "Ellison's gone." She repeated that over and over until I hung up.

Time stopped. I remember nothing except a cold numbness and a taxi driver who looked at me curiously when I threw a five-dollar bill in the little box and didn't wait for change.

I buzzed the downstairs door and was admitted at once. The door to Ellison's apartment was open. Inside, there were two detectives. First District, Homicide. Their names, I found out later, were Drosky and Buzzini. They were blond and olive-drab, respectively. A cop in uniform was standing by the bedroom door, which was closed.

Drosky and Buzzini looked at me blankly at first, then suspiciously. "These premises are closed," one of them said. I was in no mood to be stopped by official jargon and headed for the bedroom. The uniformed cop in front stepped forward briskly. In two seconds he had my arm twisted high behind my back. Firecrackers went off in my head. "Let him go," the dark one said. I straightened up, massaging my arm and lost control. They listened to my shouts with amused tolerance, then Drosky took out a little pad and started asking questions. I refused to answer until they told me what had happened. The explanation was brief. In the middle of it the crime photographer, camera in hand, entered from the bedroom. I caught a glimpse of a familiar shoe, green-and-white, encasing a motionless foot on a bed as familiar as my own.

"The deceased was discovered at nine-thirty this morning by the landlady, Mrs. . . ." the blond one referred to his pad, "Battaglia." His voice was uninflected; he might have been discussing a dead dog. "The stereo was playing loudly and disturbing her rest. She knocked, received no answer. She opened the door with her passkey and entered the bedroom. Deceased in bed, death caused by puncture wound, entrance on the right front of the chest."

He stopped and they both looked at me. "What is your relation to Ellison Greer?"

I hesitated. "He was my closest friend." They took this in and I could hear the data cards dropping into place. I didn't care. They could imagine anything they wanted to.

The medical examiner arrived, a tall man with white hair, who seemed to take charge. He joked about working on Sunday mornng — apparently it was his busiest day — then asked for details. At that point I was told to wait downstairs. The last thing I heard, as I headed for Mary's apartment, was one of them saying, "Doc, I want you to take a look at his ass."

And then, in the hall, the shock caught up with me. I stopped and leaned my forehead on the newel post while retching shook my body. Ellison murdered and the cops think he was fucked in the ass before dying. The pain coursed through me. The next thing I remember was looking up to find myself on Mary's couch and her big, handsome face bending over me. "You feelin' better, hon?" I twisted away, anguished that she should see me so defenseless. "How about some coffee?"

I buried my face in the mohair cushions and watched orange light stream through the liquid in my eyes. She moved away. Later, Buzzini and Drosky came down to ask more questions.

"Was Ellison Greer gay?" The little word sounded odd on their lips. I was feeling better; Mary had sat with me for a while, then fixed me breakfast.

"Of course he was gay," I snapped. "You know that as well as I do."

They looked at me as if they could say a lot more on that subject, then decided not to. "Where did he hang out? What bars?" It was the dark one, Buzzini.

31

Ellison wasn't much of a drinker. I thought about the Lyric Theatre on 14th Street. I shook my head. "I really don't think he went out that much. I'm not sure."

"I thought you said he was your best friend."

"I didn't see much of him this last year."

They looked grim at that. Perhaps they thought I was hiding something.

"What was his narcotics profile?" It was Drosky. I must have looked stupid because he added, "He a drug user? Heroin? Coke?"

I shook my head. "A little grass sometimes, that's all."

"That'll show up in the autopsy."

"Who said anything about an autopsy?"

"Family usually gives permission. If not we get a court order." There was a pause as they measured the extent of my cooperation. "You want to give us next of kin?"

I thought of Mrs. Greer, lying in her dark bedroom in Elizabeth and wondered if she would be able to grasp what had happened. "Can you consider me next of kin?"

"Only if you're related by blood or marriage." Buzzini stared at me. "You're not related, are you?"

I gave the address in Elizabeth.

"By the way," Drosky said, "we'll need an account of your activities last night." A little smile crept out from under the spiky hairs of his moustache. It struck me that he was probably vain about his looks. "Just checking," he added.

"Yes," I replied, wishing they would go away, "I'll be glad to tell you."

They accepted Mary's offer of a drink — each one taking the shot of whiskey neat — and grew momentarily more affable. "We had a case like this right down the street," Drosky said. He turned to his partner. "When was that?"

"Two months ago."

"Yeah, two months ago." Drosky shook his head. "The gay guys are really knocking each other off." He finished his drink. "Especially in Chelsea."

"Did you find out who did it?" I asked.

"Nah." It was Buzzini. He seemed undisturbed. "These cases are tough to solve."

They thanked Mary and left, after noting my home address. From the rear they seemed lumpy and misshapen, no doubt because of their shoulder holsters. They struck me as emissaries from another world.

The funeral was held at the same parlor where Ellison's brother had been laid out — in the chapel of the Nesbitt Funeral Home. Ellison's skin had turned gray and liverish; his nose seemed sharp as a stone axe protruding from the white silk of the casket. He was dressed in a dark blue suit I had never seen him wear. The cruelty of funerals struck me like a blow, a pagan rite designed to increase agony rather than relieve it. There weren't many people — school hadn't started yet, and most of the teachers were still dispersed — and newspaper coverage in Elizabeth had been scant.

Ellsion's mother was in the front row, her cane held between her two bony hands, looking — with her dark skin and snow-white hair — like a negative someone hadn't bothered to print. There were others from the neighborhood — dark, gentle people. And from the city myself, Mary Battaglia, Jared Green and one or two others. I hadn't heard from Hamilton Thorpe and Paul Ferrara and assumed they were still in Europe. We hadn't met up with them, of course.

They have a machine that lowers the coffin into the grave. The sight of Ellison creaking into his tomb under a garnish of yellow mums was as sad as anything I could remember — even my father's burial. I knew a portion of my life was ending — call it the second growing-up time — and I knew that whatever I was, however loving or competent, I owed mostly to the cold clay at my feet. Ellison had taught me how to survive in New York. More than that, he had taught me how to care — about my work, my world, myself. And at the graveside, enclosed in the bell-jar of my grief, I promised to unravel the mystery of his death. It was a promise that would have been better unmade and unkept.

The police investigation wasn't even half-hearted. I don't believe the apartment was visited again. I called the detectives several times — always having trouble getting through, never having my calls returned — and was given the same officialese each time. "The investigation is continuing and we have nothing to report at present." It might have been on tape.

I recalled Buzzini's casual reference to an unsolved case on the block. How thorough had their search been? Even I knew you can't enter a room without leaving behind some mark of your passage — hairs, saliva, lipstick, fingerprints. At one point the police photographer had made a phone call. Had he smudged a set of previous fingerprints? We would never know.

They refused to send me a copy of the Medical Examiner's Report directly. I had to go through the usual red tape for it. The transcript, when it arrived, shouted its obscenities at me.

"The unembalmed body is of a 35-year-old well-developed and well-nourished Negro male weighing 158 pounds and measuring 68 inches in length. There is a vertical scar in the left upper quadrant of the abdomen..."

I knew about that scar. The result of a knife fight on the way home from school, aged fourteen.

"...Cause of death. Puncture wound in the heart, bringing on internal hemorrhaging and irreversible shock. In addition, superficial puncture wounds incl. skin puncure and venipuncture..." .

It was impossible to imagine the kind of person who made a living from writing this sort of thing.

"...Time of death. 2 a.m. approx. Sunday Sept. 3. Trace alcohol. Gall bladder analysis shows no narcotic content. Toxicology testing incl. radioimmune assay and gas chromatography complete. All negative. The foregoing instrument is a certified copy of the original on file in this office, attest John O'Rourke, Chief Medical Examiner-Coroner...."

I wasn't much wiser for it. I buried it in the bottom drawer of my desk, behind the old check stubs, with the feeling that in time the report would enmesh me in some unforeseen way.

I spent as much time as I could with Mrs. Greer. After school opened it was difficult, but I went faithfully every Sunday afternoon. We didn't say much but I knew she liked having me around. I started doing the cooking for her, as Ellison had. She had lost two sons within the past year and I was the closest thing to a substitute. I don't think my physical resemblance to Ellison meant much to her. It was our friendship, our years together, that made me important. She was like one of those mother ewes who recognizes her offspring by the odor. I had the smell of time with Ellison about me.

The question of the apartment had to be settled before the end of the month. Mary relied on her rentals for a livelihood, and though she said Ellison's things could stay on, I knew we shouldn't do that. It was finally arranged that I would invite Ellison's friends to come on a Friday night to buy what they could use, and we would donate the unsold stuff to the Salvation Army.

I spent the day in the apartment sticking little price tags on everything. Several people had offered to help, thinking it would be a grisly chore, but I refused. I knew this would be my last time in Ellison's apartment, and I wanted to store up impressions against the separation ahead. As I worked I had a strong sense of his presence. These things — the sling chairs, the Signac watercolors, the Japanese screen with the white-bearded gentleman floating in golden space — were full of him. Testaments to his taste. I finished the living room, leaving the records and tapes untouched. I planned to buy those myself.

The bedroom was sparsely furnished. Just a chest of drawers, a few side chairs and the big platform bed with an elaborate headboard. Its shelving included a clock radio, the red sex-lamp and the big Random House unabridged I had gaven him for his crosswords. I started tagging the bentwood chairs first — twelve dollars each, I recall. The chest I priced at fifty dollars, thinking it wasn't likely to be sold.

I don't know what impelled me to lift the dictionary out of the headboard. We had already arranged for Ellison's few books to go to the little library on 23rd Street. Perhaps it was my fondness for dictionaries — I have a small forest of them. Or perhaps it was something else, a psychic force loose in the room. The book is heavy, awkward to use unless it's resting on a flat surface. But I opened it, riffling through it until I found the object that was looking for me. It was on the spread headed GLIM-GLUT.

It was a torn sheet form the *New York Times* Magazine section, folded neatly into fourths. I sat on the bed, resting the book on my lap while I unfolded it. It was the crossword page, with something inside it. A shiny grey plastic skin, squashed flat by the weight of the book. My eye went to the top of the torn newspaper page. Then I sat for a long time, the black letters pressing into my eyeballs while the lumber in my head moved around. *Sunday, September 3.* The *Times* hit the news-stand between 8 and 9 on Saturday evening. Ellison had probably bought it at Eighth Avenue, at the little place run by Palestinians. Approximately five hours before he had been stabbed to death.

I resisted looking at the plastic skin until I had checked the crossword. It was incomplete. The neat, square capitals didn't fill all the blanks. That wasn't unusual. I had seen him work a puzzle all week, carrying it to school, taking it out during free periods. He was like a terrier with a bone.

Gingerly, I picked up the plastic by one edge, dangling it. I turned it around slowly. It was irregular, the lower edge ragged, as if it had been cut with scissors. It was folded in on itself. Very cautiously I tried to part the layers. It gave a slight crackle. When it was all separated it flopped limply from my hand. I could see it was shaped like a sleeve or a cylinder.

Perhaps the information came from the psychic energies loose in the room, but suddenly I knew that Ellison had used this device at some point during that last night. Used it in some way I could not yet imagine.

I don't remember how long I sat there, staring into space, only dimly aware that time was passing and there was still a lot of ticketing to do. My thoughts went to the telephone several times but my legs refused to take me there. Buzzini's disinterest in gay deaths still burned in my memory. The most superficial search of the premises would have turned up the objects in my hand. There had been no investigation and there never would be. The death of a black man and a homosexual — the words drove into my head like nails — was not something high on the priority list at Homicide. Racism did not end at the grave. And what could be done about it? Who would protest? The widows and orphans and lovers of New York, carrying signs that said, "Police Unfair to Murder Victims?" Bitterness rose to my mouth, tasting of almonds. Ellison was right. They were sugar and he was salt. No matter what they said. No matter how much room they pretended to give him. I would not demean his memory by asking for help.

I struggled up at last and replaced the dictionary, then started writing the little price-tags again. I suppose I was short-circuiting badly by then, because I remember thinking, as I looked into the mirror over the chest of drawers, that Ellison had gone through it and come out all silver on the other side, serene at last.

III. Jared

Roy Renfro was talking. "I say it's time to get out of New York. Not only do they always refuse to pass a gay rights bill but the fag-bashing is getting worse. When I think of the chances I've taken. To say nothing of the danger of death by disease."

Four of us were crammed into one of the booths at Thayer's, a Greek restaurant on Sheridan Square. It had recently been remodeled from fake wood, plastic and hokey murals of the Parthenon to glass, chrome and track lighting. ("From high-dreck to high-tech," Roy had remarked when we came in.) Although Roy, his friend Peter Romagna and Jared Green were all within inches of me, I felt quite distant from the whole scene. I had been hijacked for the meal by Jared. He'd turned up at my apartment and insisted, in his abrasive way, that I join them. He had found me sitting stupidly, staring at the cardboard cartons containing Ellison's record and tape collection. It seemed impossible to do anything about them.

Jared was sitting beside me, his fleshy thigh squashed against my own. I gave him a corner-glance. His heavy face and gravelly manner hid great sweetness. Ellison used to mock him by calling him Jared the Well-Beloved. They had met during Ellison's year at Chase Manhattan, where Jared was in charge of something called Community Relations, which Ellison described as "pacifying the field hands."

"There's only one solution." Roy moved a forkful of eggplant to his mouth. "We've got to give up sex." Roy was small and blond and solid. He looked as if he had been compacted by one of those trash-reducing machines prior to being enclosed in plastic.

Jared laughed harshly. "That'll be the day. You'll just have to play Russian roulette like everybody else." His thick hand closed over the stem of his martini glass. He usually drank through dinner. Through the evening, in fact, his speech becoming more deliberate, his pauses more deadly, until he sounded like a tape running at half speed. I glanced at his profile again, at the mane of grey hair, the square forehead, the strong fleshy chin. He might have been handsome — a lion of Judah — except for his skin, which was as pocked and pitted as a cheesegrater.

Sitting so close to him, I recalled something Ellison had told me years ago. Jared had had his face flamed. The two of them had been drinking after work — recovering from the hypocrisies of the day, I suppose — and Jared had confessed to the operation. It had been done ten years earlier, when he was in his late twenties. They had burned off several layers of epidermis, the skin flaring up and curling away like seared acetate, but they couldn't find the layer of clear skin they were looking for. The lesions went too deep.

Jared had gotten very drunk as he told Ellison about it, the pain and humiliation building with the intoxication until, at the end of the evening, he had sat back against the banquette — his eyes dead moons in that scarred visage — and told the last awful truth. I remembered Jared's words now, as Ellison had repeated them to me in a voice full of borrowed pain. "And I realized they could burn and burn. Burn right down to my skull and they'd still find scars. I am the scars. The scars are me." Jared had laughed his harsh laugh then and added, "They could've gone all the way. Kept burning. Cremated me and scattered my ashes from a plane. They still wouldn't get rid of the scars. They'd only make scars on the wind. Scars on the sky. Scars on the fucking *stars*."

Ellison had gotten him home by half-carrying his dead weight through the city night. He said Jared had been like a beached whale. They had never referred to the subject again.

"Do you know what the French call New York?" Roy was still talking. "*La capitale de la terreur*. Somebody told me that in Paris last year."

"Oh for Christ's sake." It was Peter Romagna, Roy's friend and one-time lover, as calm and competent as Roy was shrill and hysterical. "Nothing's going to happen to you in New York."

As Roy started on the subject of unwarranted optimism, we caught sight of a well-know gay filmmaker, a tall hand-

38

some man of forty with peach-fuzz all over his chest, lurching along the sidewalk in full leather regalia. Roy interrupted his tirade to remark, "There goes Johnny Hutchins, look." All eyes turned. "Probably on his way to the Black Sabbath at the Hellhole. Isn't he too much?" Roy's eyes sparkled and I got the impression that the scene at the Hellhole might hold some secret message for him — if he had the courage to hear it. He slid more eggplant into his mouth then pointed outside. "Do you know I can hear Johnny Hutchins coming toward me from half a block away? I mean, all those keys and cuffs and cockrings jingling." Roy giggled. "It sounds like the entire housewares department at Hammacher Schlemmer on the move."

I found myself locked out of the conversation; as if I were in the balcony during the performance of a third-rate comedy. From time to time I touched the inside pocket of my jacket. The crossword puzzle and plastic sleeve were in an envelope. They seemed a link with reality I couldn't find here at Thayer's.

My thoughts slid back to the furniture sale two nights ago. It had gone off better than expected; I would be able to give Ellison's mother checks totaling almost a thousand dollars. His friends had been generous.

Everyone at the sale seemed to handle me with care, as if I were a depth-bomb about to go off. Jared, who bought the bureau, insisted on doing the bookkeeping. Mr. Rivkin turned up with his elegant blond wife and bought the dining-table, a Parsons, that his wife said she would "antique" — whatever that meant. As they were leaving, Rivkin patted me awkwardly on the back and said I had done a good job. It reminded me of another pat he'd given me, when I first started at P.S. 9. "Remember," he'd said, *pat-pat*, "discipline is up to the individual teacher. You maintain order in the classroom by earning the respect of the students." After he'd left, Ellison had given a mock salute and said, "You've just seen Captain Bligh of P.S. 9. *The man is dead, sir. Flog him anyway, Mr. Christian!*" Now, watching Rivkin leave Ellison's jumbled apartment, all that seemed a lifetime ago.

Mary Battaglia had brought some of her friends, the ones who had known Ellison, and there had been a sprinkling of others. Roy Renfro, I had to concede, had been especially generous, buying all the hanging prints for an inflated price. Minnie and Anson Graef, old friends of Ellison's who ran an art-supply shop near their loft in Tribeca, had bought the

Japanese screen, the old gentleman floating in golden space. A handful of teachers, now reconvened for the fall term, also turned up with their checkbooks. I was surprised, however, that Liz Garrity didn't show, though later I heard someone say she was down with the flu.

To my surprise, I found their poking around, weighing, judging, extremely irritating. At one point, quite irrationally, I wanted to shout, What right do you have to look into Ellison's things, to paw his clothes and dishes and chairs?

"Say Cord," Peter Romagna's voice was elaborately casual, "I'm a little tired tonight, why don't you take my ticket and go to the show with Roy?"

The others chimed in. A terrific troupe at La Mama, good reviews, everything. But I shook my head, pressing the envelope against my chest.

"Have you thought about taking a little time off? From school and everything?" Jared's breath was rancid with gin.

"I can't leave right now."

"The other night I heard your principal — I forget his name — say you were one of his best teachers and if you needed time off he could arrange it." Jared was being kind and in a small way I was grateful. But it had nothing to do with me.

I saw glances being exchanged and sensed they were in agreement on one thing — no talk about Ellison tonight. The envelope seemed to burn against my chest.

"Are you sure?" Jared moved his martini around. "If it's money . . ."

"I can't leave right now!" The words snapped out. I heard feet shift uneasily under the table. Roy glanced at his watch.

"Maybe we'd better . . ." he began and I knew the tone. Cop-out time. Avoid the unpleasantness. *Now*, I thought, removing the envelope and laying it on the table. They all drew back. In the sudden hush I heard dishes clattering. I opened the envelope and took out the crossword page, spreading it. I closed my hand over the plastic sleeve.

"What is it?" Roy's voice was high with distaste.

"Look at the date."

"September 3rd, so what?"

"Don't you know what that date is?"

"No I don't." His voice was petulant now. He looked at his watch again.

"It was the day Ellison was killed."

A silence followed. At last Jared mumbled, "What about it?"

I felt a slow flooding of satisfaction. They were involved now, caught up in the same web that had entangled me. "I found it next to his bed. Inside his dictionary. He worked on it the night he died. Just *before* he died, as a matter of fact."

"How do you know?" It was Peter, always cool, matter-of-fact.

"Because he bought it between 8 and 9 p.m., most likely, and died at 2 a.m. and it's more than half done. There's probably an hour's work on it. Look."

They looked grudgingly, then back at me. Another silence. Roy broke it shrilly. "Well, what in the name of God do you want *us* to do about it? What did the police say?"

"I haven't told them."

Roy's eyes grew into bulging blue marbles. "You haven't told them? Are you crazy?"

"I don't think so."

"Well you *have* to tell them!" Roy was sputtering. "If you don't tell them it's. . . it's a crime!" I felt Jared's thigh begin to jiggle nervously.

"I thought of that." Strangely, the more excited they became the calmer I felt. "I don't believe they'd do anything even if they had this. It was right next to his bed and they didn't even find it." I paused, trying to marshal some figures I had come across recently. "Do you know there were close to 20,000 murders last year? More than ten times the rate of any other advanced country? And the percentage of them that gets solved is decreasing? The police aren't even trained. They don't even know how to collect evidence."

"And you do." Roy's voice was venomous.

I shook my head. "I don't. But at least I care. That's more than they do." I glared at him. "Maybe you too."

Peter put his hand on Roy's arm to restrain him. I saw spittle collect at the corner of his wide mouth. "What about fingerprints, Cord?" Peter's question was logical. "That paper might be full of them. Now they're probably gone."

I thought of the photographer and his hand on the glossy surface of the handset. "They're not interested in fingerprints," I said. "Ellison's case isn't going to be solved by them. It's not on their calendar."

"You know, Cord, the police are trying to work with the gay community these days." It was Jared.

41

"Public relations bullshit!" My head was wonderfully light. "Besides, I haven't shown you everything. This was inside the puzzle." I opened my hand.

They reared back as if it were a snake. Roy was the first to speak. "What is it?"

"The sleeve of a plastic glove. A long plastic glove, the kind that reaches halfway up your forearm. It was cut off at the wrist. You can see it was white once." I stretched out the rolled lip, baring the white plastic.

"Okay," Jared's voice was thick but clear. "Now tell us why you're showing it to us. Instead of to the police."

I ignored his question. "I believe it was a double condom." There was a moment while they all visualized its possibilities.

"You mean two people share it?" This from Jared.

"Yeah. Two cocks. Extra friction for extra jollies."

"How did you figure that out?"

"Because there's semen inside." I stretched it. They peered at it, then at me.

"How can you be sure?" Peter asked.

"Yes," Roy snapped, "I'm sure you haven't had it analyzed chemically."

"No."

"All right then."

"Don't worry, Roy. I've seen a fair amount of dried semen in my day."

Jared, surprisingly, was on my side. "He could be right," he said.

I hunched forward. "Ellison had sex with someone using this, just before he died. Sometime during the evening, before or after he worked on the crossword. All we have to do is find out who uses this kind of thing. I mean, how many people cut up plastic gloves for sex?"

"Find out who uses it?" Peter frowned. "How would you go about that?"

I hadn't known until then. And suddenly, absurdly, it floated into my head. "We know the scene. New York. The four of us have hundreds of contacts. We could get information in ways the police never could.!"

I looked around. I was not encouraged by what I saw. Roy's lids were lowered. Peter seemed to be frozen in mid-motion. Jared was shaking his head slowly.

"Don't you see, we're the only ones who can do it!" The blood throbbed in my head. "At least we have to try!"

42

Silence.

"Or is it the old New York story? Don't get involved. Even with somebody you loved."

Roy looked up at that, his eyes almost white with anger. "That's not it and you know it. It's stupid and futile and..." he searched for the word, "...neurotic. Ellison was your colored mammy, we all know that. But he's gone now. Dead and gone. We're not going to bring him back by combing the back alleys for all the creeps and crazies and criminals. What do you think? It's our turn to get murdered? Not for Ellison, not for you and most certainly not for myself." He was bobbing up and down in his seat. "I said to Peter before we came — ask him — I said we're going to have a crazy evening with Cord. I knew it. I *knew* it! And by God I was right!"

I turned to Peter. "What about you?"

He chewed his lower lip, thinking. He seemed unaffected by Roy's outburst. At last he shrugged. "If you think you have to do it, go ahead."

Roy stood up. He was throbbing with anger. "And furthermore, I intend to call the police and tell them you're withholding evidence."

"Don't do that, Roy," Jared said, suddenly authoritative. "Cord has a right to do what he wants."

Roy glared at me. "Don't forget, Ellison was my friend too." He threw a bill on the table. "Even though you always resented it."

I started to say something but Jared stopped me with a hand on my arm. Roy left in a flurry of self-righteousness. A few seconds later Peter excused himself and followed, but not before wishing me luck. Only the smell of Roy's cologne lingered in the booth.

"He has a point, you know. You'll be the one that gets hurt from this."

"I'll get along fine," I replied. "Especially if I don't see that asshole for a while."

"Roy means well. He just gets upset if his routine is disturbed."

"You ever see the expression on a dog's face while he takes a shit? Like he had nothing to do with what's coming out the other end? That's what he reminds me of."

Jared looked reproving. "Charity begins at home. Besides, he was very fond of Ellison. And you know it."

He was right. I was being uncharitable. *A crazy evening*

with Cord. The words still stung. Because there was some truth in them. I looked at Jared. "What do you think of my idea?"

"I think it's terrible." He shrugged. "But if you feel you have to... for a while..."

"Will you help me?"

"No." A pause. "I'll give you moral support."

"That's all?"

"I'm afraid so."

I took a deep breath. "Okay. Where should I start?"

He studied the tablecloth. The scars on his face were glowing, as if he had swallowed a light-bulb. I wondered if that usually happened after the fourth martini. When he spoke, his voice was slower, wearier.

"I'd start with the bartenders. Show them that thing. They hear gossip. Check the personals in the gay press. Maybe you'll get a lead. You might..." he drummed slowly on the tabletop, "...take your own ad."

"Terrific. I can talk about what a thrill this thing is." I held up the plastic. "See who turns on to it."

He shook his head slowly. "You're really going to do this, aren't you?"

"Of course I am."

"The odds are a thousand to one."

"I don't care if they're a zillion to one."

He studied my face and I had to force myself not to turn away. "You weren't responsible for Ellison's death, Cord. Remember that. There's no reason to feel guilty." He seemed to gather himself for one last effort. "You were his dearest friend. You kept him going for years."

The corners of my eyes stung. "He kept me going too. In some ways, I'm totally his creation."

"Well," Jared's eyelids had begun to droop, "I guess we're all the creation of somebody or other."

I fumbled the plastic and crossword back into the envelope. "Will you go with me to a few bars tonight?"

He hesitated. "Just this once. After that, you're on your own. Moral support only."

"That's better than nothing," I said, getting up and putting the envelope into my jacket pocket, over my heart.

IV. Anthony

I checked the slip of paper again. West 48th Street. The three-hundred block would be between Eighth and Ninth. I knew this neighborhood — uptown flank of the theater district, monotonous block of brownstones, their facades like identical paper cutouts. The area had decayed in recent years, perhaps because of the sleaze of Eighth Avenue, known hereabouts as The Sewer. This block was halfway toward the look of a moon crater now — gaping holes and rubbish-strewn lots. I passed an addict lolling on a stoop, then recalled Preston Ware. It seemed ages ago that Ellison and I had taken our students on that basement safari.

The house I wanted would be in mid-block. I was uneasy now that the moment was here. My tours of the bars had turned up nothing so far, though the bartenders had promised to stay on the lookout. The ads I had placed had evoked a lot of vaguely kinky offers, involving rubber and plastic devices of various sorts. Only this one, from Anthony Wiggams, had referred specifically to a plastic sleeve. He had refused to go into details on the phone, had insisted that I visit him. I wasn't sure, until I stepped off the subway at 50th Street, after a long day at school, that I would keep the date.

At one point in my erratic wanderings around town, I had actually walked into the city room of the *N.Y. Times.* I had expected to find middle-aged men there; I was not prepared for the white heads and bent backs around me. It seemed like a convention of ancients. The man I spoke to was in his sixties. He had the manner of a small shopkeeper rather than a journalist — sharp, distrustful, canny.

He didn't comment while I told the story. "Sonny," he

said when I finished, "I'm sure you're telling the truth but we can't touch this story. I could give you a hundred reasons. I'll stop at three.

"First, we'd have to have a corroborating witness — a man of good character to confirm that you found these materials where you say you did. It's not a question of whether I believe you. We can't interfere in a way that might prejudice any trial.

"Second, we can't publicize materials in capital crimes that come to us from sources other than the police unless we make our own investigation. Frankly, this case isn't important enough for that. I don't need to tell you how many cases occur in New York that could lead to a legal proceeding.

"And third, I wouldn't touch it because it would mean trouble for you. You're withholding evidence. I shouldn't even be talking to you. An article in the paper would have them down on you, from the D.A. down. So you see. . ." he took a drag on a cigar, ". . .I'm actually doing you a favor. But good luck anyway." He stood up and smiled, showing a set of false choppers, and strolled away.

The return buzzer admitted me to the brownstone. A voice, high and nervous, floated down from the upper regions, advising me I had four flights to climb. When I reached the upper landing, I found a small gold-and-champagne creature leaning over the balustrade, smiling hard. He was in his late twenties. His skin was rosy, his body firm. He was wearing a shirt of coarse netting. Tawney chest-hair sprang through the openings.

"Cordell?"

"Yes."

"I'm Tony Wiggams." His flat hazel eyes flickered over me. He seemed to approve. "Well, well," he said. He led the way into the apartment.It was sparsely furnished and very clean. Bright fall sunshine poured in from a skylight. "I was so afraid you wouldn't come. When I read your ad, I said to myself, there's somebody I want to know, but the question is, does he want to know me?" Wiggams laughed lightly. "My, you certainly are tall and such good shoulders." He wet his lips and seemed lost in thought for a moment.

"I guess we're both interested in the same thing," I replied. When he looked blank I added, "Plastic sleeves."

He appeared confused, then his face cleared. "Oh yes, yes we are. Indeed."

"Do you know many people who, um, dig the same sort of thing?"

He looked around evasively. "A few. You have to be careful in New York. Who you invite into your home. That's why I got your phone number."

It was true. When I had called the number given in his letter he had asked for my own and called back a minute later.

"And I checked your name in the phone book. Cordell McGreevy. Is that your real name?"

"As far as I know."

"I thought maybe you were in show business." Wiggams motioned me to a futon and perched lightly on a wooden stool. He studied me. "Such big hands too. I hope you don't smoke. I'm allergic to tobacco."

"I do, but I won't if you prefer."

"I'd appreciate that. Sometimes people tell me they don't smoke when they really do. But they can't fool me. I have a very sensitive taste system. Tobacco smoke turns up in your cum, did you know that? Gives it a funny taste. Sort of smoky." He giggled. "Like hickory. But I'm so glad you told me the truth." He wriggled on the stool. "This is getting nicer and nicer."

I leaned forward on the futon, fighting uneasiness. Roy and Jared had been right. Definitely a creep. I measured the distance to the door. Then the crinkle of the envelope in my pocket reminded me. I made myself sit back, stretching my legs. Anthony's eyes fastened on my crotch.

"How do you feel about food?" The question was so odd I could only repeat it.

"Food?"

His hazel eyes snapped. "I'm a nutritionist by profession." He named a big hospital on the east side. "I supervise three meals a day for more than two thousand people. It's quite a responsibility." He seemed to wait for a response.

"Yes, it must be." I tried to nod pleasantly.

He looked grateful and went on. "I was drawn to nutrition because I was small for my age. Not *tiny*, but... well, you know. I don't mind now. It's all over, the hurt feelings and all. The other boys calling me Shadow or Wishbone." His voice faltered for a moment. "I'm not small now." His eyes searched mine, a question spinning up from their clear depths.

"You don't seem small to me. Not at all."

"I've built myself up through proper diet and exercise." His satisfaction was audible. He straightened on the stool, arching his back. The champagne chest-hair popped out a little more. "I've overcome my heredity. We can't all be as lucky as you." He eyed me thoughtfully and his tongue ran over his lips again. "I hope you're not into very heavy scenes."

A wave of relief went through me. Perhaps he was less eccentric than I thought. "Not at all," I said, reaching into my pocket. "As a matter of fact. . ." I took out the plastic sleeve and held it up, "I just want to know how you heard about this."

"Oh, that gismo." Wiggams looked at it with something like distaste. I waited.

"I'm sort of. . . researching it."

He looked at me sharply, almost slyly. I don't think he believed me, because he repeated, "Researching it?"

I nodded. A light silence fell. At last I said, "Would you mind telling me where you used it?"

He straightened up. "I didn't say I used it. I am merely. . . familiar with it."

"From where?"

He didn't answer. Instead he got off the stool and wandered around the room. "When I was a boy my parents gave me anything I wanted. Once I was in church — we lived in Minneapolis — and I told my father I wanted an ice-cream cone. He took me out and bought me one, just like that. Right in the middle of the service."

He stood under the skylight, the late afternoon glow reflecting in his coppery hair. I had the feeling he was talking to himself. "I went to a shrink. Here in New York. He said that was my trouble. I go through life expecting ice-cream cones." He moved toward me. "But doesn't everyone?"

It was my chance to bring him back. I held up the plastic device. "This is sort of an ice-cream cone."

He wrinkled his nose. "It's disgusting. Put it away." Suddenly he sat down, next to me. He smiled agreeably. The nostalgia trip seemed to be over. "Would you mind if I asked you something?"

I edged away slightly. "Go ahead."

"Well." He glanced away. "Are you circumcised?"

My uneasiness returned, but I replied. "No."

"Oh my." He turned and his eyes played over me excitedly.

I was aware that a contest of wills was brewing. At the same time the absurd notion came to me that I wouldn't find what I was looking for without a sacrifice. That if it was easy it wouldn't work.

"I'm going to ask you to do something. You might find it a little. . . weird. Will you?"

I crushed the plastic device in my palm. He saw my motion. "Tit for tat," he said. My clamorous breathing was audible. "Don't worry," he said, "it doesn't involve sex. You don't even have to take your clothes off."

He must have sensed my surrender because he jumped up, signaling me to wait, and went toward the kitchen — a space behind a beaded curtain. They clinked as he passed through. Then I heard some drawers and cabinets opening. At the same time I heard Ellison's voice, light and mocking, in my ear. "Who do you think you are, Nancy Drew?"

When he came back he had a saucer in his hand. There were small brown pellets in it. "M&Ms," he said. An apologetic smile formed on his lips. "I hope you haven't showered recently." When I didn't reply he held up his hand. "Don't tell me, it might ruin it."

I measured the distance to the door again. If I was going to leave. . . .

He told me what he wanted in a brisk tone, but under it I heard other things — fear, sorrow, compulsion. When he finished he gave another apologetic smile. "I told you I have a very sensitve taste system." He paused. And then, unexpectedly, we both began to giggle. A moment of madness that hit us at the same time. It was weird all right, but it was harmless. Totally harmless.

I took the dish and went in the bathroom, locking the door behind me. Each pellet — there were about a dozen — had to be coated or at least odorized. When I got through I washed thoroughly, peeling back the foreskin to make sure no chocolate had adhered. Then I unlocked the door and went back to the living room. Wiggams was standing on tip-toe in the center of the room He had an elegant form — quite perfect, in miniature. I gave him the dish. "I'll just put some Saran Wrap over this," he said, "before all that deliciousness evaporates."

"You're different from most people who put ads in newspapers," Wiggams said. "Most of them have been. . . sort of swallowed up in their thing. Nothing left over. You're not like that."

We were sitting across from each other, finishing cups of herbal tea. He gave me an enchanting smile. He seemed terribly vulnerable. I felt a sudden urge to take him in my arms and comfort him. A small white bundle of need.

"Do you go the M&M route often?"

49

He shook his head. "I try not to. But sometimes it gets the better of me. Isn't that silly?" He paused. "Nobody ever comes back. I think they're disgusted."

"That shouldn't surprised you," I said, as gently as I could.

"Last time somebody called me the Julia Child of sex." He fixed me with a humorous look. "That was really an insult. Julia Child knows *nothing* about nutrition." The humor changed to wistfulness. "I could give all that up for the right person. I mean, just go back to... regular sex."

I shifted uncomfortably. Time to change the subject. Quickly I told him about Ellison, myself, finding the plastic sleeve. His eyes were round and alert as he listened.

"I wish you'd told me the whole story at the beginning."

"I tried to."

"I cut you off. I'm sorry. I was afraid... um, you'd get away from me." The wistful look returned. "Do you blame me?"

I looked around. The room reeked of loneliness. "That's okay," I said. "Now tell me what you know."

"Okay. Every once in a while I go to the baths. On 28th Street. Very unsanitary. The Board of Health should close them down. But mostly I go for the odors." He paused, looking guilty. "There I go again. Anyway, time before last, I met a little man who had that thing in his hand. He showed it to me. Sort of demonstrated. It didn't really turn me on so I said no thanks. Even though he was rather attractive." He paused. "I think he was a foreigner."

I could feel my pulse jumping. I leaned forward.

"Next time I went, a week later, he was there again."

"What night was that?"

"Monday. That's my night off. I have a feeling he's a regular."

"Could you call me if you run into him again?"

Wiggams smiled coquettishly. "I have a better idea. We could both go together. Next Monday."

I considered for a moment. "I'm game."

"Maybe... maybe we could have dinner first?" His hazel eyes deepened.

Dinner with Wiggams was something to be avoided. I told him I usually worked late Mondays. He looked at me skeptically. "I wanted to make it up to you."

"It's not that I don't want to, Tony, just..."

"I know, you have to work late." A hint of the old snappishness returned. He stood up. I did too.

"I'll call you later in the week. We'll make plans."

"I don't think most people appreciate the sensual quality of food." He was talking to himself again. "Most of them are just lab technicians! They wear sterile smocks and gloves!"

I moved toward the door. It was time to leave.

"This is the last time I'm going to do this! Answer an ad!"

I was almost at the door.

"My patients need me! They don't know what good food is! All those Spanish people... rice and bananas, that's all they eat! Rice and bananas! They're old at thirty-five!"

I moved out to the landing. The stairway, below me, looked fragile and unsafe.

"I've got them, why do I need somebody like you?"

There was no answer to that. I looked back only once. He was leaning over the balustrade, his face hurt and vacant and angry, all at once. "Take care," I muttered inanely.

I was halfway down the stairs when his voice reached me. It was urgent and shrill.

"Cordell! Cordell!" I stopped, craning upward. He leaned over, his features contorted. "Next time we're going to use Jello! You hear that? Jello! In the bathtub!" I turned and hurried down while the echoes pounded off the walls. "JELLO-O-O-O!" they gave back. "JELLO-O-O-O-O-ooo-ooo-oooo!" As if an obscene wind had gotten loose from its cave. I escaped into the street but my ears rang all the way to the subway.

V. Avery

"Try one of our Schimmelpfennicks," Paul Ferrara said, pushing a box of slim cigars across the coffee table. "We went all the way to Amsterdam to get them."

I took a cigar and bent my head for Paul to light it. The mild flavor, vaguely cinnamon-like, grazed my tongue pleasantly. Perfect for after dinner, a splendid meal that had consisted of watercress soup, curried veal and *oeufs á la neige*. Paul cooked the way he refinished furniture and designed interiors — with small, precise gusts of competence. No grand passion, just a reliable excellence. Enough to get the work done exactly.

I looked at him, sitting alongside me on the loveseat, his aquiline face composed. He was a monument to good sense and self-control. Nothing was out of place, not in his life, not in his apartment, probably not even in his bedroom. At least it appeared that way, and I was adept at spotting false fronts.

Hamilton, sitting in a Barcelona chair across from us, reached for a cigar. He was getting bald now — the short grey hairs on the sides of his scalp glistened in the lamplight — but he was still trim and attractive. "No, we didn't, Cord," he remarked. "We were going to Amsterdam anyway to see the Van Goghs. We think they're a smash."

As usual, he was speaking for both of them. I remembered what Ellison had said about them. "People like Hamilton and Paul give homosexuality a good name." We were walking out of the lobby of their art-deco building at the time. He had jabbed the air, then snapped his fingers. "They make it easier for everybody else," he added.

"More coffee, Cord?" Paul leaned toward the crystal-and-chrome coffee-maker, the plunger type. I shook my head.

"You should have been with us," Hamilton resumed. His voice still had a slight Texas twang, even after twenty years in New York. "You would have loved it. Especially the Ile du Levant. Wouldn't he, angel?"

"Oh, definitely."

"We'd never been to a nudist colony before." He grinned, looking mildly shocked. "It completely restored us. We were knocked out from touring."

"It's so marvelous lying in the sun with nothing on. It's completely different from what you'd expect." Paul's voice was a high counterpoint to Hamilton's.

"But it's not like the nude gay beaches. It isn't sexy. In fact, there's a kind of unwritten law — don't stare. You wouldn't want to stare at most of them anyway." He tapped some ash from his cigar. "I was amazed at the variety of pubic hair on the women."

"Cord doesn't want to hear about that." Paul looked slightly alarmed.

"He doesn't mind. I always thought women's pubic hair was kind of standard. You know, except for some color differences. But my God! I've never seen so many different shapes. Scraggly and thick and high and low and wispy and . . . everything you can imagine. From a single fern to a whole forest."

Paul drew in his breath. "Why don't you tell Cord about Madame Branca?"

"That's just the first day or two. After that you notice people who are *wearing* clothes. You wonder what on earth they're doing with all those colored ribbons." He paused. "We're going back next year. And you're going with us, right, angel?"

Paul looked at me. "That would be marvelous," he said.

Perhaps we all thought of the same scene just then — the send-off at Kennedy, just after Ellison had cancelled our rendezvous. I know I did. Because there was a moment of discomfort, then Hamilton started speaking again too quickly.

"Madame Branca was our landlady. What was the name of the pension?"

"Mer et Soleil."

"Yes, Mer et Soleil. She was closing up at the end of the season — just about now, I guess — and going to live with her daughter in Macon. She said she'd seen enough naked bodies to last the rest of her life."

"You know the type, Cord," Paul added, "probably raised by nuns and never let her husband see her in the nude."

"We got some beautiful provincial pieces — she had them right in her salon. For a good price. Wait 'til you see them."

"We'll probably have a showing when they arrive. A vernissage."

I looked at them again, their faces alight with enthusiasm and kindness. A phrase of Henry Miller's came to me — a phrase meant to be ugly and demeaning: "The interior decorator type of homosexual." I wondered what he would have made of Paul and Hamilton.

Paul stood up and began clearing off the dining table. His movements were quick and birdlike. Hamilton squinted through the cigar smoke. "Don't bother, angel, I'll do it later."

"Oh, it'll just take a minute. Then we can all go out on the terrace. There's a full moon tonight."

I had the feeling these were ritual remarks, offered every evening. Or maybe all day long in the shop. Paul buzzing around like a bottled fly, Hamilton sitting placidly, master-minding things. In some ways they mirrored a straight marriage — splitting up the chores and roles. Or was I merely stereotyping them? It was really far more complicated. If Paul was the domestic and creative one, then why did Hamilton spend every Saturday cleaning the apartment, doing the laundry and shopping for food? If Hamilton was the more extroverted, aggressive, why was Paul so much better at bargaining — a shrewd, tough buyer of used furniture? No, I thought, as we gathered up smokes, ashtrays and coffee cups and moved to the terrace, theirs is not a straight marriage nor a gay one — but simply a good one, trading off strengths and skills, connecting in ways which destroyed all stereotypes.

Out on the terrace, under a light that turned the sky-scrapers of midtown into gleaming constructions of silver foil, I listened to Hamilton talk about their plans for a branch in Key West. It seemed so simple and rational. Even though I knew half the rationality came from Paul, humming inside as he cleared off the dining table, I felt a twinge of envy. My own planning seemed fuzzy by comparison, disfigured by a heavy load of emotion. The events of the last weeks seemed absurdly out of place on this moonlit terrace.

Roy had been right. I had come up against an army of equipment freaks spread out over the five boroughs. None of them — except for Wiggams — had actually produced the plastic sleeve I was looking for. But my ad, apparently, was enough to release fetishes and fantasies galore. There was a nervous overweight man in Brooklyn who talked about a "plastic envelope" that turned out to be a nylon sleeping bag. There was a loud Broadway type, middle-aged with plucked eyebrows, who referred to a plastic suction cup (the nozzle of his vacuum cleaner).

But last night had been the worst. Someone on the other end of the wire whispering about a new kind of rubber container. When I got there, a handsome young man wanted me to give him an enema.

In a way, this failure was encouraging. It proved how unique was the device Ellison had used. On the other hand, its very rarity was leading me up blind alleys. My dreams had been scary for weeks. Blood and death in strange combinations. And school! Some days I stumbled around, half-asleep, coming out just long enough to scream at the kids. Jesus Gongora asked me last week why I was mad all the time. What could I tell him? That I was mad over love and death and skin-color? Or that I was mad at myself, furious over something I didn't quite understand?

"Are you okay, Cord?" I came out of it to find Hamilton looking at me, his face silver-plated in the moonlight.

I shook my head. "I'm sorry. I'm not very good company tonight."

"You don't have to put on an act with us."

"I was hoping..." I smiled ruefully, "...I wouldn't be a drag tonight. First time together since you got back."

"You weren't a drag. You never are. You're one of the people we care about."

His kindness barreled across the terrace toward me. "I know that, Hamilton."

"Why don't you come and stay with us for a while? We have a folding bed we can set up for you."

I shook my head. "Thanks anyway." For a moment I thought I would tell them about my amateur sleuthing. Even though Jared and I had agreed not to. They wouldn't have minded the extra burden. But it seemed so hopelessly out of place in their lives. Besides, what did I have to show for my efforts? A food freak and a bathroom Romeo? I couldn't bring myself to do it. Luckily, Paul stepped out on the terrace just then. Another minute and I might have changed my mind.

"There! All cleaned up. Can I get anyone anything?"

"Not a thing, angel. Sit down." Paul pulled a wrought-iron chair next to Hamilton's and sat down. He put his hand on top of Hamilton's. I saw his fingers tease the black hairs on the back.

"You know, Cord, we felt terrible about coming home too late to help you or Ellison's family. We were upset for a long time. We still are."

"That's right, Cord," Paul echoed.

"I was wondering how you found out. Did Jared tell you?"

"No," Hamilton replied. "It was the switchboard operator at your school. I asked to leave a message for Ellison and she started to cry."

"Marta. She was crazy about him."

Hamilton's voice was almost buried in his throat. "Everyone was. He was a beautiful guy."

We sat silently for a few minutes. At last Hamilton said, "Since we're on the subject — did the police find out anything?"

"No."

"You know they came by here."

"I'm surprised. They've done almost nothing. They must have found your names in the address book."

Hamilton looked uncomfortable for a moment. "I assume they know the whole score."

I thought about Drosky's request to the doctor. "Are you kidding?"

"We weren't much help."

I felt the bitterness coming up again. "They were probably glad."

Paul looked startled. "What do you mean?"

"Ellison's case wasn't important enough." I started to choke on my anger.

"No!" from Hamilton.

Again, I thought about the proof I could give them. "They didn't do a fucking thing. In fact, they were bragging about the murders they couldn't solve, gay people killing each other. If they came by here it was a fluke. Something to look good on a report. I'm positive they didn't do a thorough job of checking out the address book." I sat up straight. "It wouldn't have done any good anyway."

"Why?"

"Because. . ." I shrugged, "whoever killed Ellison didn't know him. At least didn't know him well enough to get in his address book. It was some freak! I'm positive!"

"Did you tell the police that?" Paul's voice was light and antiseptic, an antidote to my rage.

"I don't remember what I told the police. I only saw them once. That morning. And now they won't tell me anything on the phone."

Paul leaned forward, his pale skin glowing. "You mean to tell me the police aren't doing everything they can to find out?"

I laughed. "The police depend almost entirely on paid informants or eyewitnesses. Detective work isn't their bag. Takes too long. And it's too expensive. Besides, Ellison wasn't important enough to bother with. At this point he's just a scribble on the police blotter!"

I saw them trade glances and I could almost read the message: cool it. I turned away, embarrassed at embarrassing them. They didn't deserve this. The dinner party had been their gift to me. And I was on the verge of ruining it.

Just then the door buzzer rang. I could almost see the relief washing over them.

"He's early,' Paul said, getting up. "He said he had to work until eleven." He stepped quickly through the French door.

Hamilton didn't reply, just dragged on the stub of his cigar, the strong bones of his cheeks highlighted by moon-shadow. For a moment I thought I saw a fleeting look of annoyance, but whether it was caused by my outburst or by the arrival of a visitor I didn't know. Paul returned, followed by a tall young man in a clone outfit — flannel shirt, levis, work shoes.

"This is Avery Gilmore," he announced. I stood up to shake hands. Then Avery went over to Hamilton. They brushed lips lightly.

The white night illuminated Avery Gilmore clearly. He had dark blond hair and skin the color of clover honey. His eyes were brown. He seemed to concentrate light in himself, as if he were the focus of a hundred candles.

"I'm sorry I'm early," he said, sitting down. "First time I've been early any place in years. I can go out and come back if you want."

"That won't be necessary," Hamilton smiled.

"What would you like?" Paul, ever-watchful, hovered behind Avery.

"Some white wine would be great. We had a joint in the cutting room and wine would be dynamite."

Paul left. As Avery and Hamilton talked, I examined him. He was about thirty. The planes of his face were flat, his nose strong and bumpy. With a three-cornered hat he might have been a younger version of George Washington. But his eyes were soft and his voice was gentle. He had that low, uninflected way of talking, as if the slightest emphasis would jar his listener, imprint an authority that wasn't intended. But under the flat voice, the blurry gaze, I had the feeling Avery was all together. When Paul returned with a glass of wine, I watched him move it very slowly and precisely to his lips. His big bony hand wrapped it completely. He sipped without haste; I had the feeling he'd sip it that way in front of a firing squad.

As the conversation progressed, I gathered that he was a filmmaker. He hired out as a cameraman — he had his own equipment — but was trying to make a feature. He had already optioned a script by someone he knew from film school, but had failed to stir up any interest at the major studios. Now he was going the friends-and-relatives route. I wondered if Hamilton and Paul had coughed up some cash. They could probably afford it.

If he knew I was staring at him, it didn't show. Maybe he was used to attention. But I couldn't help feeling there was something happening between us. I was positive when he got up and walked to the edge of the terrace to look at the moonlit city. He moved with an easy elegance, a swinging grace I had seen only once before in my life. My heart dropped on a plumbline as I recognized that bouncy walk. It was the walk of a man who heard music all the time.

"Really great," he murmured, looking at the spray of lights on the horizon.

"Don't you get the feeling sometimes," Hamilton gestured expansively, "that New York is the center of the world? I don't care what anybody says, it's still the most exciting place. You know why? Because the most exciting people are here. The best. Look at the four of us!" He wheeled around, extending his arms. "Where else is everybody so interesting?"

Avery raised his eyebrows mildly. "Santa Fe. Frankfurt. Kyoto. There are interesting people everywhere."

Hamilton grinned. "Then why did you end up here?"

Avery shrugged. "More money here."

"That's exactly what I'm saying. The best people collect where the money is. And the power."

I cut in. "You sound like a real provincial, Hamilton. Everything begins and ends with New York."

"Come on, Cord. You're the biggest admirer for miles around."

I thought of all the places Ellison and I had visited together. I had always been glad to get back to New York.

58

"The giant wart," Ellison called it. But it didn't matter. There really wasn't any place else. Avery was looking at me, waiting.

"Yeah," I admitted. "I'm hooked. A lifetime sentence. Love and hate — twice as strong as love or hate separately." I let out a little sigh.

Did I read disappointment in Avery's glance? Had he decided I was dull or unadventurous? It was an unpleasant notion and I brushed it away. But it kept returning, during the next hour, as the conversation veered from one topic to another and Avery almost never looked at me.

I was surprised, then, when I got up to leave, that Avery announced he would walk me to the subway. Paul glanced at Hamilton just then, his dark lashes fringing his eyes so that I couldn't read the message. Were they glad or sorry? Had they planned it this way? I wouldn't have been surprised if Avery had been a blind date for me. It was just in their line. I thought I read satisfaction on Hamilton's face — the matchmaker kind — as we stood at the door, but I wasn't sure.

Paul took a heavy wool djellabah out of the closet and handed it to Avery. It was white, banded with black and grey vertical stripes. Avery dropped it over his head, then stood very tall and tent-like.

"Love it, just love it," Hamilton said, "don't you, angel?"

"Where did you get it?" Paul asked. "It's a Berber pattern. Have you been to Morocco?"

Avery shook his head gravely. "I got it in Mendocino." He cocked his head. "You'd be surprised what you can find in northern California."

As they talked, my eye was caught by a framed notice next to the door. It was a certificate. As usual, unable to resist the lure of printed matter, I sneaked a glance. It was an award — "First Prize to Hamilton Thorpe and Paul Ferrara for their costumes at the Captain's Gala aboard the QE2," followed by a date. I'd never seen it before.

I turned to find Paul's eyes fixed on me. The irises were black pools. It struck me that he looked very tired. I gestured toward the wall. "You didn't tell me about this."

"Oh," he wrinkled his nose, "it isn't anything."

I frowned. "I didn't even know you came back by ship."

"One of those fly-and-sail deals." It was Hamilton, cutting in. "We went over British Airways, came back five days on the QE2. Boarded at Cherbourg. Very relaxing."

Avery was waiting for me. I hugged both Hamilton and

Paul. I hope I conveyed some portion of my affection in those hugs. The evening had been a gift — a thoughtful, considerate gift.

They stood in the open door while we waited for the elevator — their arms around each other, faces glowing. Just as the elevator clanged upward, I thought to ask, "You didn't tell me what the winning costumes were."

Paul laughed. "We just put some things together. Bedspreads and all. Camped it up."

"Don't believe him. He's proud as can be. That's why he framed the award."

And then it was time for a last smile and wave.

Avery and I kept in step for a few blocks without saying much. He seemed very exotic in his djellabah. He put up the hood when we reached the street, folding back the edge so his face was framed. He didn't seem to notice the passersby staring. He wore it as if it were a cloak under desert stars rather than a bit of urban extravagance. But our silence didn't seem to separate us. Maybe Avery was one of those rare types who can be silent without disappearing. He seemed to be sending out little signals, like a star. With his hands, his eyes, the swish of his robe. Nothing had to go into words.

When we reached 53rd Street, my subway stop, he asked if I'd like to see his place. He lived two blocks further down Third Avenue. I didn't hesitate long. About three seconds. I had a sudden feeling that Avery might erase some of the sights and sounds of the last few weeks. Soiled events that would disappear with a certain kind of treatment. "You know," I added as we continued walking, "I like it when you don't talk."

"Oh, I talk sometimes," he said lightly, without moving his head, "but right now I'm seeing you in a viewfinder. I got my head filled with that."

When we got upstairs — he lived on the fourth floor over a liquor store — he unlocked the door and said gravely into the dark, "This apartment says hello to Cordell McGreevy." By the pale tints of the neon signs below I saw a large airy space filled with leaves. When he turned on a lamp I saw that the living room was crowded with giant plants. It looked like a rain-forest.

Avery went to a high white cage, shaped like a miniature mosque, and opened the door. He put his hand in and two yellow finches hopped aboard his finger. He tossed the birds in the air. They sped around the room like gold bullets, dipping toward our heads on every circuit, squeaking with pleasure. "Just like dogs," he said, "gotta let 'em out for exercise every once in a while. Care to turn on?"

I shook my head.

"Mind if I do?" He took a joint from a leather box on the coffee table. After he had lit up and inhaled a few times, he remarked, "Hamilton and Paul are probably pissed at us."

My head buzzed briefly. "Why?"

"I was going to make it with them tonight. That's what I was invited for. Didn't they tell you?"

"No."

"Yeah." He nodded quietly and took another drag. "They dig threeway sex. They're pretty good at it too. All smooth and easy — kind of choreographed. This is the first time I've been up there since they got back. And you were there." He hissed in more smoke and air. "I think maybe they expected you to be gone by eleven o'clock. But I was early."

I recalled Hamilton's fleeting look of annoyance when Avery had first arrived. And his later — so I thought — expression of satisfaction at his matchmaking. I had misread all the signals. "I thought you were an old friend of theirs."

"If you call four months old. I met Paul on Central Park West, just before they left for Europe. Hamilton was sitting in the station wagon waiting. I guess you could call Paul the bait." He looked at me evenly. "I don't have anything against threesomes."

"I don't either but Hamilton and Paul. . ." I paused, trying to fit this new information into everything I knew about them. But it wouldn't go. I must have looked stricken.

"Its their thing. So what?"

"Nothing, only. . ." I couldn't explain it to him, nor to myself. He watched me for a moment, then moved his head toward me, tilting it. I kissed him, running my hand over his shining hair. It seemed a very precious act. He pulled back after a moment, his brown eyes luminous.

"This is gonna be nice," he breathed.

I heard a celebration of wings overhead. As he finished the roach I tried to put Hamilton and Paul out of my mind. With only partial success. It wasn't until Avery stood up and started to unbutton his flannel shirt that they disappeared. A stretch of skin, bare shining skin, was what I needed most — and my sense of survival came to my rescue. I began to strip.

61

Avery was stunning in the nude. His chest was wide and flat with dark hairs that curled like wings from the gully between his pectorals outward to his nipples. His chest slimmed to a small waist, where the dark honey of his skin gave way to a strip of dazzling white. I began to explore him with my fingertips, over the bony shoulders and soft hair to the navel and below. I passed my fingers around his buttocks and traced the tantalizing crevice between them. He stood very quietly, letting me discover him.

"You're so beautiful," I whispered.

His eyes flickered into focus. He studied me for a moment. "Don't move," he whispered, "I want to change the lighting."

He stepped behind one of the plants, a huge ficus, and touched a control. The table lamps faded and two spotlights on a ceiling track came on. They threw a circle of light where I was standing. I found myself bathed in a hard brilliance. The leaves at the perimeter of the room became a dark wall. We might have been standing in a clearing in the woods.

Avery stepped inside the clearing. His body whitened, its edges sharpened and hardened. The lines and gullies of his chest deepened. He seemed to have moved into high relief.

"My God, you look like you've just been carved out of marble."

"You don't mind?" He smiled his low-key smile.

"Fantastic," I said. The noise overhead increased. The birds were excited by the change in lighting too.

Avery came up to me and slid his lips slowly down my chest. He kept going, sinking to a kneeling position. With agonizing delicacy, his tongue moved over my cock, wiggling down the underside, coming back to circle the tip with a ring of fire. I stroked his hair. I had the feeling we were joined inside a nuclear explosion.

"Easy," I cautioned at last, "or I'll finish right now."

He looked up. For the first time I noticed that two of his front teeth overlapped badly. I felt a surge of tenderness for Avery with crooked front teeth. He was not perfect after all.

I hunkered down and rested an arm on each shoulder. "Let me see your ass," I whispered. His eyes went smoky for a moment then he leaned over and gave me a long kiss, a kiss I perceived as the finest of gifts. Then without a word he stretched out, face-down, on the shag rug.

I straddled him, aware of the harsh light playing on my chest and shoulders. I ran my hand down his back. The skin burned like golden fire. Suddenly he snaked out his arm and opened a drawer in the coffee table. He gave me a tube, then pillowed his head on his forearms. He seemed to be half asleep.

When I was ready I eased myself in slowly, oh so slowly. At last, with a shudder that passed from my body to his, I was home, lodged to the hilt in the luscious chambers of Avery's ass. He gasped, then went limp with acceptance. We stayed that way for along moment. Then, lifting with care, I began to move. Avery found the rhythm with me, slowly at first, then faster, writhing and rearing, crying out as we moved together, and then an incredible release, my back arching while fountains exploded and I heard Avery groaning as he reached his own climax.

Afterwards, silence except for the sound of wings overhead. I kissed him midway between his shoulder blades, where a thin film of sweat had collected. I could see the artery in his neck throbbing. I tried to withdraw as slowly as I had entered, anxious to lessen the inevitable moment of pain. Even so, he winced.

I don't know how long we lay on the shag rug, my arm shielding my eyes from the light. I was dimly aware of the need to get up and wash. But I couldn't. At last the whirring noise broke through to me. I moved my arm. I couldn't see the birds.

"What a racket," I said.

Avery rolled over on his side facing me. He watched me carefully. "Ri-ight," he breathed.

And then suddenly, unaccountably, I knew. Knew with a cold sense of betrayal and loss. "That noise," I said. I sat up. "It isn't the birds, is it? Is it? *Is it?*"

He kept his eyes, huge and steady, on mine. "Uh-uh." He shook his head slightly.

The wires in my head trilled. "What is it?" I went to grab him but he motioned to one of the plants and I turned. I couldn't see at first. I had to squint against the light to make out the metal barrel and the glass lens. Round and shiny and deadly as a gun. "Oh no!" I cried, turning away quickly, "you made a movie of us having sex!"

"Just a little vCR," he said in his even voice. "You didn't want all that to go to waste, did you?"

VI. Nino

...a huge red sun, big as a blood orange, filling the morning sky, pushing aside the blue like crumpled paper, coming towards me, nearer and nearer, starting to suck me into its shiny depth.... suddenly a knife in my hand, tearing through the orange tissue, making it run like the yolk of an egg... terror, tossing anguish, sirens, firebells....

The telephone took me clear to the other side of the dream. I got up, flooded with relief at the stay of execution, then stumbled into the living room — over the clothes I had dropped last night when I got home from Avery's — in reflex obedience to the summons. The voice was familiar, light and high. I didn't have pleasant associations with it.

"Remember me, Cord?... I hope you're not angry... Hello, Cord, are you there?"

"Who... um, who is this?"

"Don't tell me you don't remember." An aggrieved pause. "Tony."

"Who?"

The voice was higher now, wounded. "Tony Wig-gams."

Oh God. The room came slowly into focus. I massaged my forehead.

"I wanted to... um, apologize about going off like that the other day. I really felt awful afterwards. I just went all to pieces when you walked out. I don't blame you for not calling. Even though you promised."

I walked the phone to my pants and fished out a pack of cigarettes. "That's okay..."

"Well, you'll be happy when you hear what happened. Last night at the baths."

64

It took me a while to zero in on the new information — or was it old? *The baths. Tony Wiggams at the baths.* I began to recollect.

"I ran into him again. Last night. Are you there?"

"Yeah... yeah."

"Well, it was just like I predicted. He's a Monday night regular. A hairdresser probably. And I did you a favor. A very big favor."

The cigarette was lit, the fog had cleared. "You did?"

"A favor I wouldn't do for just anybody. I told you I liked you." A pause, filled with expectation. "He had that plastic thing with him. Tucked in his towel. So I was thinking about you and your friend, what was his name?"

"Ellison."

"Yes. And I thought, I'll just see what this is all about. So I went to his room with him, and we started in. And after we were hot, he... um, he put it over both of us. Snapped it right on. And you were right, Cord. It's a condom. A great big condom. A condom built for two!" I heard a moist giggle. "It was marvelous. I never felt anything like it."

"Did you ask where he got it?"

"Of course I did. What do you think I am? As soon as we finished and he took it off, I asked him where he found out about it. If he created it himself or what. But he had a thick accent and I don't think he understood me. He was in a big hurry for me to leave. You know what it's like at the baths."

"You didn't find out where he lives or anything?"

"Well hang on! Just before I left I told him I loved it and I wanted to do it again. We made a date for next Monday. Though I really shouldn't go, it's so unsanitary in that place."

The disappointment made me sag. "You mean you made a date for the baths? He'll never show up."

"Well don't be too sure. After I told him how much I enjoyed it, he relaxed a bit and told me his name is Nino." Wiggams paused. "I have a feeling he'll be there. He was really kind of sweet. Just waiting for someone to take an interest in him. He told me he liked me." And then petulantly, "Some people do."

"I really appreciate..." It was difficult to find the words.

"Oh that's okay," Wiggams's voice was cheerful. "It was the least I could do after all that. Of course I'll have to go with you next Monday. To point him out."

After I hung up, I went to the kitchen and put on some coffee, fighting the absurd feeling of vindication that rose to my throat. There was really nothing to get excited about. A vague lead, an unknown person who might or might not show up. Nothing certain. Just a slight breach in the anonymous wall of freakdom. But my warnings didn't help. I couldn't put down the feeling of triumph. I don't think it even had much to do with Ellison at this point. Ellison had receded to a certain point, rather remote, where he stayed — embalmed and perfect like a mummy. Strange as it sounds, he was no longer the main motive in my search. What I wanted most — let's be honest — was to be right.

I stood by the stove, staring at the coffee-maker for a long time. Yes, I was on an ego trip to prove Roy and Jared wrong. A feeling of self-disgust came over me. My needs had taken precedence over Ellison's — even posthumously. As they had done, I suddenly reminded myself, in life.

When the coffee was ready I took it to the bathroom and set it on the hamper. The face in the mirror was not reassuring. The skin under my eyes was a smudgy purple, the color of a Caribbean sunset. There were five parallel lines on my forehead. With a G-clef and some notes it might look like a bar of music. But there was something else under all the lines and discoloration. A new wariness. Or toughness. Had my journeys to the end of night, over the last month, given me a thicker rind?

As I shaved I thought about the closing scene with Avery last night. When I turned from the camera barrel, my chest and shoulders freezing with shame, he had been as cool and mild as ever. I forget what came out of me — obscenities, outrage, it doesn't matter. All the disappointments of the past weeks spewed out in a froth of rage and betrayal. A betrayal drama with Cord McGreevy as star. But there was some justice on my side. He had no right, not really. But he didn't agree. He listened to me, his head cradled in the crook of his arm, not blinking, and finally, after I quieted down, he said, "Don't sweat it, Cord. I'll destroy the tape. No problem."

"That's not the point," I flung at him. "You had no right to do it in the first place. It's rotten! It stinks!"

He seemed genuinely puzzled. "Why?"

"Because it's an invasion of privacy, that's why."

"I don't dig it. It's my privacy too. I don't mind."

"My God, don't you understand? We don't even know each other, really, and you film me fucking you."

"Is there supposed to be something wrong with fucking me?"

"No! Yes! I don't know!"

"I'm not gonna use it anywhere. I mean, like you're not going to end up in a feature."

"How do I know?"

"You can trust me."

"Trust you? I trusted you when I walked in here and look what you did!"

"Man," he shook his head, "if I'd known you were gonna get this upset I would't have done it. I got thirty or forty cassettes already and this never happened."

"You got *what?*"

He regarded me calmly. "Go wash and I'll show you."

He did. In the bedroom there was a bookshelf full of cassettes, each in a shiny yellow plastic case with a name lettered on its spine. Also a date. Lionel. Jeremy. Kermit. Some with women's names. Clarissa. Pru. Janet. Some with two names. Pete and Hilary. Temple and Popeye. Millie and Tom. My eyes ran over them unbelievingly.

"About twelve hours," he remarked. "With you I got twelve and a half." He looked at me. "Keep it at twelve," he murmured. "I guess you got some hang-ups about sex."

"Hang-ups?" I barked. "If you call this wanting to fuck in privacy a hang-up, I guess I do. This is... this is..." I was sputtering with indignation, "...you're a voyeur! That's what! If there's one thing I didn't figure you for, it's that."

A look of quiet amusement crossed his face. "Could be," he said, "maybe that's why I'm a filmmaker." He batted his eyes. "Seeing is my thing." He followed me back into the living room. "Like, I'd like to see *you* again."

"Invite me to the première." He winced and I was sorry, but it was too late. He went to the recorder and ejected the cassette. Then he slipped it in the case and handed it to me. As I weighed it I had the feeling something fine had turned into ugliness. "Thanks," I said, "I'll keep it so you won't be tempted."

"I won't be tempted," he said. His fine three-cornered face was impassive. I knew he was telling the truth.

Our goodbyes were brief. Strained nods at the door. We were suddenly strangers — all the more painful for the intimacy that had gone before. We both wanted it to be over as quickly as possible.

On the E train going downtown I held the container in my hand. I knew what I should do — toss it into the first incinerator I could find. But I didn't.

When I got home I put it in the back of the top bureau drawer, behind the socks and handkerchiefs. I would destroy it tomorrow. Or the day after. It had been a great evening, but it had turned sour. And the evidence had to be destroyed.

And then, unexpectedly, I thought of a line from Thomas Wolfe, one of my favorites: "For if a man should dream of heaven and, waking, find within his hand a flower as token that he had really been there — what then, what then?"

Yes, the cassette had to be destroyed. But not right away.

Minnie and Anson had gone to quite a bit of trouble for their guest of honor. The Graef loft, a vast space with a ceiling of stamped tin and serried ranks of columns, was filled with food, paintings and people.

I saw a few who had been at the sale of Ellison's furniture, including Mary Battaglia, who gave me a long hug. Jared Green was there, moving ponderously toward me, martini in hand. He filled me in on the purpose of the event.

Not that I needed much of a clue, since the walls and partitions of the loft were hung with gauzy soft-hued paintings of . . . eggs. In tempera, acrylic, gouache and oil.

"She says it's nature's only perfect form," said Jared, his voice lumpy with irony. He nodded toward the artist, a tall rosy woman of thirty with jet-black hair. Her eyelids were a metallic blue, reminding me of dragonfly wings. He paused to sip his martini. "I think maybe if she got pregnant she'd start painting something else." He studied me. "How's the sex research coming along?"

I should have known better than to tell him — known he would pooh-pooh it. But I couldn't resist.

As I detailed my meeting with Wiggams, suppressing the more lurid portions, and his subsequent encounter at the baths, Jared kept his dark eyes trained on me. "And so," I finished up, trying to pump some enthusiasm into my voice, "I've got a date next Monday. It's a break, the first real break."

When he spoke, his voice was patient and parental. "The chances are ten to one he won't show. Those bath-house types never do." He glanced around the room, filled with men and women in plumage brighter than any tropical aviary. "Besides, what can he tell you? He probably read about the device in some freakbook. Or saw it in a store that sells kinky sex things. Or got it tenth-hand from a hustler off the bus from San Diego."

"That's no reason not to follow it up."

"Well, it's okay to go, but don't expect too much."

I could feel irritation welling up. "I thought you were going to give me moral support. This doesn't sound much like it."

A pause, then a sigh. "Well, I'm just trying to get a note of. . . reality into all this. I know you pretty well. I know what an attraction. . . fantasy has for you."

My irritation flowered into anger. "Everyone goes through life with needs they don't lay out on the table every minute!"

He changed the subject. "How're things at school?"

I thought of the difficulties of the first few weeks of the term. It's amazing how sensitive ninth graders are. I subscribe to the theory that children are fully human but of a different race. They are not ignorant; they simply know other things. The Little People. My students understood what was going on inside me as clearly as if they had read about it in our current textbook. ("Mr. McGreevy and Mr. Greer were *friends*.") And they made allowances. Most of the time. But it wasn't fair to ask them to keep it up, week after week.

"School is okay."

"Really?"

I couldn't remember the last time I'd heard Forest Murmurs in class. Not this term, certainly. Not since Ellison.

"Yeah. Really."

I turned away. I'd had enough Jared for a while. There were more interesting conversations waiting around the room. I wanted to ask Mary if she'd rented Ellison's flat. I hadn't really caught up with Minnie or Anson. And I had to speak to the guest of honor. I cast about for something intelligent to say about eggs.

I was saved from this dilemma by a tug on my leg followed by a chant: "Up your brain with Gravy Train! Up your brain with Gravy Train!" Followed by squealing laughter.

I looked down. She was about ten years old, with freckles and pigtails and several pounds of aluminum alloy on her front teeth. "Hello," she said, "I'm George."

"You're George?"

"Yeth."

"Well, George, I'm Cord."

"I know what a cord ith. Ith eight feet tall, four feet wide and four feet long."

"You must have a terrific arithmetic teacher."

She shook her head. "My mother told me." George pointed at the guest-of-honor. "Thath what we burn every winter."

You burn me in your stove every winter?"

Another squeal. "Yeth."

Our conversation must have caught Minnie's eye or ear because she came over looking, I thought, rather worn — her slender face a little more lined, her chestnut hair dyed a little less artfully. She and Anson put in long hours at their art supply shop south of Canal — a cut-rate place favored by freelancers — and besides that, were active in the gallery world. They were, Ellison had told me when he introduced me, born do-gooders. "They do good and they expect everybody they know to do good, so next time bring your work-clothes." He'd sneered in that mock-tough way of his, then added, "They'll have you cratin' pictures before you can say Toulouse-Lautrec."

"I hope Georgina isn't bothering you," Minnie said.

"I'm not Georgina, I'm George!"

"We seem to be having gender problems," I murmured. .

Minnie looked fondly at Georgina-George. "What does your mother call you, dear?"

"She calls me thweetheart." The freckled nose wrinkled in distaste.

Apparently we ceased to be of interest to the child because as Minnie asked me about myself, she wandered off. I had always liked Minnie Graef, from the afternoon last spring when Ellison took me to their shop and we sat amid the crates in the store-room sipping tea. There was something both domestic and brisk about her, as if she could bake bread and spot talent with equal ease — which in fact she did. I suppose she must have been quite beautiful once, in a spare, Hepburn-like way, but now, in her early fifties, she had been refined down to sinew and bone and darting blue-gray eyes.

I was aware of their concentration as I told her how hard it was to teach knowing Ellison wasn't nearby. "So," I wound up, "it's been a drag. More than that. A disaster."

Her face registered sympathy, but before she could speak, Anson came over. I've always liked him less than his wife — a bald, stooped, taciturn man. Someone whose dreams have died and left a slight rancidity behind. He peered from Minnie's face to mine, almost suspiciously, as if we'd been talking about him. I saw Minnie stiffen and her hand, with its delta of swollen blue veins, go to her throat. For the first time I wondered if she was afraid of him.

"The punch is all gone," Anson said.

"I'll get some more," Minnie whispered almost guiltily and, with a tap on my arm, veered off. I was left looking at Anson's bald dome, which was reflecting one of the mounted spots. I moved to his left.

"What's new?" he asked. "About Ellison?"

"Not a fucking thing."

"I thought I heard you talking to Minnie about it."

He was looking at me intently, his mouth curled as if he'd just bitten a lemon. It occurred to me that, for all his bohemian surroundings, he was probably a man who didn't have much use for homosexuals.

"We weren't talking about the case. We were talking about school."

"Oh." He looked sideways, then back at me, as if he might catch me off guard. "You hear from the police?"

"They did an autopsy, then put everything back just where they found it. Mrs. Greer didn't even notice."

"And?"

"Nothing. No clues. They've filed it away. Case #4193, in case you want to call."

I don't want to say he looked relieved at that — relief is too strong a word — but he looked as if he didn't much care that the investigation was over. Another phrase of Ellison's came back to me, uttered soon after we had left Graef Art Supply that first day: "They are the best — they pulled me through a very rough period after my divorce."

Was it possible he was referring to Minnie and not to Anson? That I had misheard or misremembered? Anson excused himself and went off to help Minnie with the refilled punch bowl. As I watched him cross the room, crab-like, I decided to give him the benefit of the doubt — at least for now. They had both been friends to Ellison; by extension, they were also my friends.

"You wanta thee thomething?"

I've never been able to resist an offer like that. "Sure."

She led me confidently through the gaps in the crowd, reminding me how quickly the Little People master any maze of grown-ups.

"Look," she said.

It was a little puppet theater, faded and in disarray, but

somehow still alluring — on a chest of drawers in a corner of the bedroom. The cloth puppets, like crazy gloves, were lying inside and out. "What ith it?"

I felt a tug of delight. I'd once made a booth for marionettes and put on a show with my sister. "It's a Punch-and-Judy show!"

I tried on one of the gloves — a fierce soldier in a Hessian helmet — and wiggled my fingers menacingly. Then I helped George-Georgina put on another glove — a fat woman with a tiny rolling-pin. We fenced and feinted for a while, then I said, "Let's put on a show!"

She was all for that. We'd just managed to move the cardboard stage to a table, however, when she squinched up her nose. "She's calling," she said.

I hadn't heard a thing — a mother's voice might be too high for my ears — and started lining up the rest of the puppets.

"Oh!" The exasperation rippled through her body and ended as a stamped foot. "Jutht when we were having fun!"

And then I heard it — not high, but a mellow, almost dark voice. "*Sweet-heart!*"

I looked toward the direction of the main living area. When I turned around, I was alone. Only a squeaking and scuffling behind some sliding doors let me know that George-Georgina had moved to the clothes closet.

"Did you see my daughter?" The guest of honor, breathing hard, was in the doorway. "I knew I shouldn't have brought her."

I wrestled with my conscience only for a moment. I really had no right to interfere. Still, I felt like Benedict Arnold when I raised my chin slightly in the direction of the closet.

George-Georgina made an exit worthy of a demonstrator in the good old days — first she went limp, then she screamed, then she clutched at every article of clothing within reach. There were a good many within reach, which meant that when her mother finally hauled her out of the closet and back to the living area, half the wardrobe was strewn about. "Thank you!" she called at me, still struggling with her daughter, "I think she's over-tired."

A diminishing wail, like a fire-siren, contradicted that statement. I turned my attention to the mess.

I'd got about half of it back on hangers when a voice thin as a knife cut through my reverie. "What the hell are you doing?"

I turned, guilty without cause, to find Anson Graef staring at me, his eyes slitted, his stooped, emaciated frame tense. "The kid... she was hiding in here..." the foolishness of the scene just ended froze on my lips. *Did he think I was snooping through his wardrobe?*

"Put that down, please. The party's in the other room."

Stung, I threw the cotton shirt in my hand onto the bed. Any further explanation was beneath me. The broad blue-and-white stripes of the shirt burned into my vision. Then I turned and went into the living room.

Jared was in front of an acrylic — not really focused on it, just pretending. He seemed to be swaying slightly.

"I'm leaving."

He turned fuzzily. "Already? I thought we might go somewhere for a bite."

"Forget it."

He peered at me, frowning. "Is anything the matter?"

"Anson Graef. This is the last time they'll see me around here."

He called after me several times as I walked across the room towards Minnie. I really couldn't leave without a word to her.

"Promise you'll keep in touch." I murmured something, brushing her cheek. She smelled slightly of turpentine. Then, aware that Anson was in the doorway to the bedroom, watching me out of the corner of his eye, I walked to the exit door.

It was only when I reached West Broadway that the striped shirt stirred in my memory, releasing — what? Something old and unpleasant and best forgotten. I put it out of my mind, along with the rest of the evening. No, they wouldn't see me in Tribeca soon again.

The famous bath-house was a squat, hunched building in the garment district, whose tailors and furriers it had once served as a *schvitz*. Inside the smoked-glass doors, eleven carpeted steps led to a vestibule with a wide check-in counter. The men behind it were a surly bunch, especially this one, who looked like Edward G. Robinson, cigar stub and all. I'd spotted him before. In fact, he was one of the main reasons I hadn't been here in years — since before the fire that had killed almost a dozen patrons. I didn't like doing business with thugs.

As I dropped my watch and wallet in the oblong box I looked around for Wiggams. He'd promisd to meet me here in the lobby. Only a burly Puerto Rican guard was standing by. A vague depression tugged at me — suppose Wiggams didn't show up? Suppose this was just a little game of get-even?

I shrugged off the treacherous thought and, key in hand, headed for the second floor. Room 206. Wiggams had advised me that the top floor, the third, was best — reserved for the heavy-sex crowd. My contact — I searched my memory for his name but it had disappeared — always took a room at the top. Well, I thought, ascending the stairs, I'll just be a tourist.

The attendant, an elderly black man with a sleepy air, was waiting for me. "This way, sir." He led me around a corner and down a corridor, lined with cubicles. Overhead, small bulbs gave out a faint red light. "Here y'are." He tossed two towels on the bed, deposited a paper-cup of lubricant on the table and handed me the key. I tipped him and closed the door.

The cubicle was a graffiti artist's dream. The metal walls were crammed with crude figures in every imaginable embrace. The only thing they weren't doing was kissing. The last place I'd seen graffiti this impassioned was on the subway.

My eyes were adjusting to the gloom. I began to strip, hanging my clothes on a hook that had been integrated as a genital outcropping in a complicated three-way. Again I wondered if Wiggams would show up, then tried to recall his description of the stranger. Almost nothing came except, this time, his name. Nino. What should I do? Go around asking people if their name was Nino? A sense of futility, topped by despair, returned. What on earth was I doing here? I thought of Jared's warnings at the Graef's party last week. "Chances are ten to one he won't show." And suddenly, down to the marrow of my bones, I knew he was right.

There was only one way out from these thoughts — through the door and into the hall. I knotted the towel around my waist, dimmed the light and stepped outside. Several men were strolling around. They looked at me, invitation in their glance. I nodded, smiled, walked on.

I entered the dormitory area, a space with low wooden partitions and about three dozen beds. At the far end I could see a group of men gathered around one of the beds. I went over.

Two figures were on the bed lying spoon-fashion, back to front, under a sheet. Only their heads were visible. The one behind thrust and gyrated slowly, the one before swayed to the same rhythm. The covering sheet gave a strange grace to their movements, making them fluid and even, their limbs flowing

74

like water. I thought of the stone draperies that cover a Greek statue, draperies that define the hidden torso with their flutter.

But when the man standing next to me — a paunchy type wearing horn-rims — reached out to grope me I moved on. The sight of the screwing had excited me but I wasn't ready for action.

I walked around the second floor, looking for Wiggams, looking for Nino — whoever he was. Nothing. Then one flight up to the famous third floor.

Perhaps because it was Monday night, the area seemed uncrowded, almost deserted. I suspected that the heavy-sex crowd turned up on the weekend, that Monday was stay-home-and-recover night. Only a few doors were open.

In one a young man was kneeling, head-down, on his bed, his ass cocked invitingly in the air. The can of Crisco sat just behind, in a circle of light. He must have seen me through his thighs, upside-down, because he jiggled his butt. A tremor went through my groin at the sight of those perfect orbs, but I moved on.

In another room a young black man, thin and ghostly under chains he had hung from the ceiling, sat motionless. A dog-collar encircled his neck. As I watched, he massaged his tits, pulling them out and around as if they were tassels. He gave me an encouraging smile. I smiled back and moved on.

A couple of people were standing in front of an open door at the end of the center corridor. I peered over their heads. A man cased completely in leather sat on the bed, facing the door. A soft leather helmet covered his head — cut out only for eyes, nostrils, mouth. In his right hand he held out, motionless, a funnel. The funnel was connected to a rubber tube that ran to his mouth. Over the bed, above him, was a carefully-lettered sign: URINAL.

I don't know how long I stood there, converting this sight into signals that my mind could apprehend, because suddenly I was aware of a tug at my arm. "He's here," a warm familiar voice breathed into my ear.

I turned, having trouble with the focus of my eyes. "Who's here?"

"Who?" Wiggams screeched. "Who we came here to see before you got carried away by the human pisspot!"

The people around us moved away. We had broken the spell. I looked into the cubicle again. Not a movement, not the flicker of an eye. The funnel was steady.

"Are you coming or not?"

I wrenched away and followed Wiggams down the central corridor to the back of the floor. Now that the moment was here I found myself panicking. What would I say? More to the point — what would I *do*? Some participation would be required. I thought, with sudden pain, of the place I had found the plastic contraption. Next to Ellison's bed. All my associations with it were filled with horror.

My speculations were cut short. At the end of a corridor, leaning against a steam-pipe, I could see a short square man. His heavy shoulders and thick chest were furred with hair. He was almost completely bald. We walked toward him.

"Nino." When Wiggams spoke his name his black eyes darted from side to side. "This is Cordell." Now the black eyes were scurrying over my face, body. Nino was terribly nervous. He looked behind me, down the corridor, as if calculating the escape route.

I tried to sound easy. "Good to meet you."

"Yais." A brief smile revealing even white teeth.

"I told Cordell about you. About what a good time we had."

Nino's eyes danced around some more.

"Did you . . . um, bring the thing with you?"

Nino hadn't understood. "The . . . gismo." Wiggams made a stretching motion with his two hands. Even he, I could see, was getting nervous. "Plas-tic," he said at last.

A glint of recognition came into Nino's eyes. He nodded slightly. Wiggams pointed to me. "Show him."

Nino didn't move. He looked petrified. To break the awkwardness I said, "Why don't we all go downstairs for a cup of coffee?"

It was a mistake. Nino started to move toward us, past us. "You go. I come not now. Later."

Wiggams put a hand on his arm. "He doesn't really want coffee, Nino. He wants to go with you."

A knowing smile slowly took shape on Nino's face. He stopped, looked at me again, longer this time, lewdly. Then he turned toward Wiggams. "You not like? Again?"

Wiggams smiled smoothly. "All fucked out, Nino." He spoke again, more slowly. "Tired. Fin-ished."

Nino looked at me again, his heavy eyebrows lifting into little gothic arches. "Where he's room?"

"Two-oh-six." I held up my key.

"I come. You go. I come." He waved his hands, urging us away. I repeated the room number. Then Wiggams and I left, walking downstairs in silence. At the door to my cubicle, Wiggams stopped. He wrapped his towel around his middle more tightly. "He's all yours. I'm going down to the steam room."

My anxiety returned. So much depended on this. "Stay," I whispered urgently. "We'll both talk to him."

"Uh-uh." Wiggams was very firm. "He doesn't want to talk, believe me. There's only room for two in that thing. Three is definitely a crowd." He looked at me and I thought I read satisfaction in his eyes. My discomfort pleased him. "Have fun," he murmured and swept off into the red twilight. I entered the room, closing the door behind me.

I sat on the bed, wondering how long it would take Nino to show. To get up his nerve. If he did. In another moment I was sure I'd let him get away. He wouldn't be coming at all! He'd just wanted to get rid of us! I jumped up and reached for the door, then pulled back. He was already half scared off. If I chased after him he'd probably disappear for good.

As I pondered, I became aware of scuffling noises next door. Low cries, gasps. I glanced at the intervening wall. Amazingly, a hole had been gouged out of the metal. Someone must have brought a hand-drill or auger with him, packing it along with the poppers and Lube. Nothing could stop some faggots, not even a steel wall.

Where was Nino? My nerves were taut; I could feel sweat collecting in the small of my back. The noises next door were getting louder. It sounded like rutting walruses. I fought against my curiosity — and then gave in. I moved along the bed until my eye was to the wall. Two figures were moving in a slow tableau, cocks at the ready, mouths moving, arms and legs interlocked. They were wrestling or making love — or both. I pulled back, listening for footsteps in the hall. Nothing. Nino might have left the building by now. My heart thudded in my chest. I had messed up. Let it slip through my fingers, the one link to Ellison's death. . . .

I clamped my head to the partition again. The murk, the dim light, the slow motion — it might all have been taking place in an undersea grotto, washed by tides, where half-human creatures had drowned in the act of love.

There was a tap on my door. Dizzily, I stood up, then went to the door and opened it. He looked left and right, then

77

sidled in, closing the door quickly. His right hand was closed over something. I sat down weakly on the bed. He peeled off his towel.

Nino's chest-hair broadened and deepened into a wild matted undergrowth around his groin, a glinting grove of pubic blackness. In the center, white against the dark, was a small hard stem.

"You like suck?" he whispered. I didn't answer. "Good suck," Nino declared. The organ waved, a determined prong.

I took a deep breath and motioned toward his closed fist. "What's that?"

The fist remained closed. "First suck," he commanded.

I bent down while Nino watched. I was having trouble getting my breath. "More better," he said urgently. When I looked up his face was clamped into tight concentration, his eyes dark. "You no good," he said at last.

I lowered my head again but surprisingly, after a moment, he pulled my face away gently. "Look," he said. It took me a moment to see. A piece of plastic, coffee-colored. An exact duplicate.

"Where did you. . .?" I started, but Nino was slowly, expertly, swinging my legs, pushing me back on the bed, easing himself alongside. His chest-hair, coarse and wiry, scratched me. His hands began smoothing my groin. The voice in my ear was deep and tender. "*Bello, bello,*" he murmured. The words, the deft movements of his hand, the sights I had been witnessing, had their effect on me. Nino's hard furry body rotated slowly against me and I felt myself relax. Suddenly he doubled down and tongued me expertly, stopping from time to time to measure the results. Each time he looked up and smiled. "Is good," he repeated. I arched my back as the warmth crawled upward. I felt as if I were being eaten by an oyster. Finally Nino raised himself and moved over me so that both organs were parallel. He made a swift motion. I felt the plastic fit over us like a warm wet hand. Nino, with a sigh, lowered himself, his weight on me, encircling me with his arms. He began a gentle thrusting with his pelvis while his lips brushed my cheeks, lips, hair. I felt the room slip away, the walls move outward, as I focused on the exquisite sensation in the center of my body. It felt as if we were plowing a warm sea together, oaring to some channel of unimaginable delight. Nino kept up the delicate movement of his pelvis, rocking me in a cradle of pleasure without beginning or end. On and on it went, a to-and-fro motion that lapped at my nerves, and then slowly, almost imperceptibly, his rhythm speeded up and I felt myself sliding into a dark wet center, a black hole where I might suffocate, and with a cry I clutched his back, pressing into him as the rhythm washed me into the vortex and I felt myself sliding and tumbling into a roaring blackness, a blackness that blinded and deafened and healed. . . .

I became aware of Nino's quiet body, a dead weight lying across me. We had subsided at almost the same instant. The rush of air between us, as he shifted off, seemed an intrusion of something cold and undesirable. He fumbled in the dark and the plastic device was stripped away. I heard nothing but the sound of our breathing. It had been quite a trip.

I turned to look at Nino's profile. He looked like old pictures of Mussolini. The same dome, an ostrich egg. The same heavy eyebrows and short beak. His wrist was pillowing his head. The bristles under his arm smelled of burning rubber.

"You like?" His teeth shone in the dark.

"Yes."

"I make."

"Who. . . where. . . did you find out about it?"

"Frain told me."

Things were coming clearer now. The room was moving back into focus.

"Maybe I can be your friend too."

"I see you here. Next week."

"No. I don't like it here. Dirty. Your house."

His lashes brushed downward. I saw his stomach tense. I changed the subject.

"Where are you from, Nino?"

The smile again. "Livorno. You know Livorno?"

"No."

"Pisa? Tower?" He leaned his hand slowly downward. "Livorno near Pisa."

"Oh sure. Your friend in Livorno made this?"

"No. Here. New York."

It was coming now. "Who? Maybe I know him."

Nino shrugged. My throat jammed. I twisted away, then turned back to find him observing me carefully.

"I go now." He struggled to a sitting position, then turned and looked down at me. He ran his hands over my chest, down my stomach. "Beau-ti-ful," he murmured. He kissed me lightly, then reared back. His eyes were huge and hungry. A vast immigrant yearning poured over me. Then, to my surprise, he sat back and lifted his forearm, bulging the muscle on the inside. "Strong," he said, his eyes sparkling, "lifting, alla time lifting."

"Lifting what, Nino?"

"Pans." He tapped himself on his chest fur. "Sauce cook." He named a famous French restaurant on the east side. "Make me strong." He proffered the forearm and I felt the rock-hard bulge.

"Wow."

The huge eyes searched my face again. "You gotta frain?"

I shook my head as slowly and sincerely as I could."Not now," I said.

"Beautiful boy, no gotta frain?" He was testing me, trying to read my face, his own half-averted.

"No, Nino. Not now."

The silence was heavy with unsaid things. He looked everywhere except at me. Then very quietly: "You like come my house sometime?"

"I'd like that a lot, Nino."

Another search, his eyes darting from the corners of the room to my face and back again. "You come my house Monday. Restaurant closed. I fix dinner."

He kissed me again, very gently, and repeated the invitation, with the address. I felt like shouting but I only whispered, "I'll be there. I'll be your friend."

He stood up, wrapping the towel around his waist. At the door he paused for a long moment. I had the feeling he was wondering if he'd made a mistake. But he only said, very simply, "You my frain now." He closed the door gently, as if on a fragile object.

I don't know how long I lay there, in a suspended state, warding off thoughts as if they were blows. I didn't want to explore any of the presences in the room. I wanted to keep my mind, my recesses, clear.

Suddenly I was aware of the oppressive odors of the place. Musk and sweat and oil and amyl nitrite. Attar of sex. For a moment I couldn't breathe. Then I struggled up and started to dress.

I was almost ready to leave when I remembered the scene next door. Numbly, I wondered if they were still at it. My eyes went to the peep-hole. It took a moment to locate and when I found it my stomach wrenched. The hole had been plugged with pink tissue-paper. They knew I was watching! At some point they'd become aware of me! I finished dressing, throwing on the clothes as rapidly as I could and left without looking for Wiggams. All the way home, the word stuck in my throat like a fishhook. A word I had thrown at Avery with such casual self-righteousness. *Voyeur.*

And I had always hated hypocrites!

VII. Liz

It had been one of those days when mass mischief infects the kids. I noticed it in homeroom, right off. The Spanish kids knotted into a tight group by the radiator, spitting out their machine-gun vowels, the girls dominant as usual, the boys grinning at the obscenities, their shoulders stiff. If they kept on with the Spanish, it meant they were into their pride thing — not a good sign. Three Asian boys, usually so docile, beating on their desks, their smooth brown faces crinkled with anger ("She discriminated you!" Kim snarls at his friend). Then two of the best students, Billy Athanasius and Jerry di Valli, spilled a bottle of ink on the floor and stepped in it, making blue Sporto footprints across the floor. They looked at me, a defiant glitter in their eyes, spoiling for a scolding. I didn't give it to them.

Then a mild revolt in my slow-reader class. Mitchell, a huge soft black boy, refused to read aloud. Murmurs of support, encouragement, from the back. "I don't give a shit about no mother-fuckin' goat," he whined, dropping the Aesop on the floor with a bang. The class drew in its collective breath, gleeful. Luckily, it was time for the TV. I turned on the set and watched them sink into offended passivity.

When the day ended I slumped in my wooden chair, the backache special, and wondered if I could take another year of this. Ellison's absence pained me like a wound. A vast emptiness echoed through the building. It was the kind of day we would have celebrated the end of — with a restaurant meal or standee tickets at the Met. A little present to ourselves. I knew what the evening held now. Doped-up dinner in front of the tube. The thought of calling Avery occurred to me. I played with my cup full of red pencils, considering. It would be good to see him. But I could feel the forces building on the other side. Pride. Self-righteousness. I couldn't — not yet, anyway. Much as I would have liked to tell him about today. He would have understood.

I was at this impasse when Liz Garrity turned up in my doorway, a smile on her plump face. "Coffee?" I lurched up, grateful, and followed her down to the faculty room. I hadn't seen much of her since the term started. She seemed to be keeping to herself. No doubt she missed Ellison too. I recalled our crazy expedition to Coney Island, how generously she had treated the kids to food, how she'd masterminded the putsch that got Ellison on the Cyclone.

"Did you have trouble today?" she asked. She'd put three teaspoons of sugar in her coffee. "My kids were rotten. Skunk rotten. I could've killed every one of them." Her voice was piercing. She balled her small hands into fists.

"The worst I've ever seen." But I couldn't help smiling at her. She was made like the letter S — bulging in front and behind — and when she was angry she swelled up comically.

"I told 'em, yes I did, I was gonna whack their little bottoms. Jesus. And Rivkin still hasn't signed my requisition for construction paper. Every time he sees me he hides. I'm goin' in his office and grab him by the balls and I'm gonna say, Rivkin, either I get my construction paper or you give me combat pay." She exploded into wild whooping laughter.

She was really very pretty. A Rubens type — improbable blond hair, rosy skin, vast secret bulges. Suddenly it occurred to me that Ellison had probably given her the brush-off at some point. When? How?

"I mean, how can you teach art if they won't give you the materials?"

"I guess you're worse off than me. I got my materials. Only trouble is, no one's interested in reading them."

"Interested? No one in this school's interested in anything except screwing around in the boiler room."

"Are you speaking of the students or the faculty?"

"Cordell, honey, I am speaking about *both.*"

"That's news to me."

She looked at me sharply. For an instant she seemed critical, almost hostile. "Everybody knows you're a professional virgin." She must have read the tightening in my face because she caught herself quickly. "That's all right. We love you. Just don't keep it up forever."

"I'll try," I said dryly.

Her eyes, bluish-gray, roved over me thoughtfully, glinting again. When she spoke, her voice had the same edge to it. "What do you do for fun? All by your lonesome in Greenwich Village?" She pronounced it Green-witch.

I hesitated, annoyed. Dumb questions always annoyed me. I thought momentarily of telling her the truth. I wouldn't be the first teacher in the city school system to come out. But suddenly it seemed too complicated. I couldn't add that to my other difficulties, at least not now. "Being a virgin is a full-time job," I replied at last.

She reached over and patted me. "Don't mind me. I got a big yap. Just a dumb hick from South Dakota."

Her smile seemed sincere. I was puzzled for a moment, then my irritation faded. She was like a melon — tough on the outside, soft and sweet on the inside. I wondered if she was taking out on me some of her anger at being rejected by Ellison. "I don't mind you. In fact, I kind of like you. When you're not coming on like the queen of the Amazons."

She whooped at that. "I *am* the queen of the Amazons. Can't you see? I only got one boob!" She covered one of her ample breasts and whooped again.

This broke me up. When I recovered whe was grinning like a demented duck. I had the sudden feeling she was several people in one large package. "I like you, Cord," she murmured. "You're a gentleman. Nobody likes gentlemen any more but I do."

"I like you too, Liz." I hoped it wouldn't give her any ideas. I stood up. "Come on, I'll walk you to the subway."

"And golly!" she whooped, "I might even ask you to carry my books!" I laughed. A Dakota girl as done by Martha Raye.

The subject of Ellison didn't come up until we were nearing the IRT, housed in one of those buildings, in the mid-Broadway island, that looks like a cross between a latrine and a Greek temple. And then it led to one of those strange coincidences that happens so often even in a city of eight million. Liz had spent the summer in Italy, doing sketches, she said, for a production of *La Serva Padrone* at Covent Garden. She had accumulated so much outsized junk by the end of August — books, prints, sketch pads, props — that she had to cash in her airline ticket and come home by ship. She'd travelled on the QE2 out of Southampton.

I hardly knew why I asked. It was one of those automatic questions. A reflex. "Two of my friends came back on the

QE2. Hamilton Thorpe and Paul Ferrara. You didn't cross paths?"

"Hamilton and Paul!" she shrieked, clutching my arm. "I helped them with their costumes!"

I grinned. "The ones they won with?"

"Yes! Last night out. Paul used my gold choker for a head-band! Isn't that an absolute riot?"

"I've known them for years. Ellison did too."

She glanced at me quickly at that, her eyes glinting again. "Do tell. We could have compared notes. Creamed you both. Dug out all your dirty little secrets. Their costumes were brilliant. Simply brilliant. Did they tell you?" I shook my head. "They came as Aristotle contemplating the bust of Homer."

"Which was which?"

"The older one, the one with no hair. . ."

"Hamilton."

"Yes, Hamilton. He was Aristotle. I helped him with his hat. I wangled a toque from one of the chefs and cut it up and dyed it. You know, big and floppy. Over one eye. And Paul was Homer. We draped him in purple velvet from his shoulders down. Rice powder on his face. Frizzed hair. Perfect. They got a standing ovation. It was the perfect end to the trip."

"I wish I'd been there."

"I didn't see them after that. Funny." Her voice became softer. "They didn't turn up at customs Saturday morning. Where were they, that's what I'd like to know." She caught herself, becoming more elaborately casual. "It's none of my business, I guess. Maybe they were. . . they were just trying to avoid me."

"I doubt that."

"Do you?" She looked away and I couldn't see her face. It was hard to believe she'd be hurt by such a thing. I made a mental note to bring them together.

I'm slow in some ways and I didn't think of it until I was in the middle of a dumb private-eye show on the tube, hours after I'd handed Liz her books and waved goodbye. The notion spread through me like a foul gas, constricting my throat. *Was it possible that Paul and Hamilton had been here the night Ellison was killed?* It was strictly a matter of dates.

We'd had the pre-term faculty meeting the week after Labor Day, the Wednesday and Thursday after Ellison's death. Liz had attended — I remembered all the hoo-haw about the outfit she wore, a long blue robe dotted with silver stars. It was something you'd wear to a gala at the Met, not a dreary talk in the school auditorium. Everybody had complimented her. If she'd docked on a Saturday morning, as she said, then it had to be either the Saturday of Ellison's death or one before. . . .

I stood up and looked around the living room, trying to focus on the prize certificate I had seen in the Thorpe/Ferrara apartment two weeks ago. There was a date on it. *What was the date?*

She was in the phone book under Garrity, E., on West 68th Street. She answered with a long windy hello.

"Liz? This is Cord. Cord McGreevy."

"Well, well. Tired of being by your lonesome?"

"Listen, Liz."

"I *am* listening."

"I wanted to get something straight about your crossing. On the QE2."

"Shoot."

"What day did it dock?"

"I told you. Saturday."

"I mean, what day of the month?"

"Oh. It was Labor Day Weekend. You want the exact date?"

I didn't need it — not now — but I wanted time to think. "If you don't mind."

"Wait a minute, I'll get my passport. It's stamped."

The phone tapped down on a hard surface.

"Here it is. U.S. Immigration, New York, New York. Admitted September 2. See, I wasn't lying."

"And it was in the morning? You sure?"

"Sure I'm sure. I had my hair done the same afternoon. Got all the sea crud out. What's this all about?"

"Just curiosity."

Her voice was bubbly. "You checkin' up on Paul and Hamilton?"

"In a way."

Her voice became tiny and falsetto. "I won't tell 'em."

After I hung up I turned off the TV. I was trembling, shaking like laundry on a line. Why did they lie? Why did they *have* to lie? Hamilton had said they'd arrived too late to be of help with Ellison's death. Not true — but why?

I pressed the question down as far as it would go, into the deeps of my mind, but it bobbed right up. This one little fact didn't fit everything else I knew about them.

Other questions linked hands with the first. Why had they made such a point of telling me about Marta Jones, the switchboard operator at school? Establishing an alibi? But that was foolish. The docking of the QE2 was a matter of public record, easily traced. A phone call, pretending they'd just arrived, was no alibi at all. Any detective with half a brain could have uncovered it. If he'd wanted to.

That started another link-up. Should I tell the police about this? The thought of sharing anything with Drosky and Buzzini was distasteful. They would blunder into the lives of Hamilton and Paul like bulldozers. And there might be some simple explanation. Something that had nothing to do with Ellison. Didn't I have to give them the benefit of the doubt? Didn't they deserve that?

The sound of the phone was a temporary reprieve. It was Jared, insistent on a dinner-date. Instead, I told him about Liz and the ship. He grunted several times as he listened. When he asked for confirmation I told him about the passport.

"So you see," I concluded, "it's all documented. What I can't understand is why they lied. It was so goddam unnecessary."

I could hear his raspy breath at the other end. "There might be something you don't know anything about."

"Like what?"

"They were held up at customs and didn't get home 'til after midnight."

"Come on, Jared. Labor Day weekend is the busiest time of year. They push you right through. If you're bringing in drugs, even, that's the best time to do it."

"Well," he rummaged around for more arguments, "they might have gone right out of town for the weekend. Without going home first."

"Then why did they give the impression they weren't even in the country? That they were too late to be of help?"

"I don't know."

"Okay. Neither do I."

More heavy breathing on the other end. At last, "Maybe your girlfriend is making all this up. For some screwed-up reason of her own."

That was too ridiculous to answer, but I did anyway. "Tomorrow I'll go to the library and look up the *Times* for September 2. Ten to one it'll show the QE2 docking. She talked about the costume party. They had the damned certificate on their wall. It all checks out."

A long sigh. At last, "Listen, Cord. Do you believe Hamilton and Paul had something to do with Ellison's death? Stop and think."

"No, I don't."

"Then why don't you respect their... their..."

"Lie."

"All right, their lie. Respect it enough to let it alone."

"You're telling me to overlook it for social reasons."

"Not for social reasons. For reasons that are... mutually beneficial. Do you realize? If you get them involved with all this shit you'll wreck their lives. And what do you think that will do to your own peace of mind?"

"Not much."

He harrumphed softly. "Seems to me that's pretty shaky already."

"I wasn't thinking about police," I countered. "I'd already ruled that out. I was thinking of... confronting them with what I know."

"You can do that. But you might lose their friendship. Do you care?"

"Of course I care."

"Then give them the benefit of the doubt. Trust them, Cord." His voice was juicy with sentiment. "They *loved* Ellison."

I hung up, my skull throbbing. I was angry at being reasoned with. And I knew all about Jared's brand of logic. Ellison used to deliver samples of it when they were working at the bank together. How many times had I heard Ellison, his voice light with mockery, saying, "The eek-well opp-or-tun-i-tee group met for lunch again today!"?

I remembered one example. The group had been making plans for a trip to Atlanta for a conference on hiring practices. But Ellison said he hadn't been able to hear their words over the sound of breadsticks breaking and celery snapping and chicken being sucked up. His eyes had blazed as he talked about it. "And I realized these people are doin' what they've been doin' for centuries. They are dining out on the carcass of the American black man and black woman. Only now they call it Affirmative Action and Equal Opportunity!"

And then his fingers went off. *Snap-snap.* I had listened, trying to bridge to his anger, but helpless to share it, really.

"And then it hit me," he went on. "These personnel people... they aren't egalitarians. Hell no. They're *egaliticians*! They're in the *equality racket*!"

88

A moment after he said it, his anger subsided and he sputtered with laughter. "That was so-o-ome meal we had." He shook his head. "Sight better than a fatburger at McDonald's."

Jared the Egalitician. Well — perhaps he was right. Up to a point. Hamilton and Paul had loved Ellison. And he had loved them. I recalled the Saturday morning tennis games Ellison and Hamilton had played, winter and summer, indoors and out, for the last year or so. I used to make fun of Ellison for getting such pleasure out of knocking a flap of padded cotton around a court. But he couldn't be laughed out of his games. "Brotherhood time," he used to say. "You're jealous 'cause I got more than one white brother."

Jared was right. I couldn't confront them without losing their friendship. There was no room for that kind of suspicion. But still... the question balanced in the smoky air of my overpriced closet. Why?

I decided to erase it with some music. There was no question about which. Rosa Ponselle. The record Ellison had played for me that first night, so long ago. His all-time favorite.

I dragged out the cartons of records, still unsorted, from the corner of the room. The one I wanted was the last one in the case. I slipped the disk from the jacket, then from the liner. As Rosa Ponselle began to unreel her golden line I dropped to the floor, stretching out in front of the stereo.

It was a reissue, the sound fuzzy, but underneath I could hear the strong true voice, a living fossil from 1929. The *Casta Diva* from *Norma* is many things, but most of all it's a monument to hypocrisy, sung to the moon, most chaste of goddesses, by a priestess who has committed fornication. Neoclassic nonsense, of course, but it has always given the aria an icy undercurrent for me. It struck me that the ancients should have endowed hypocrisy with its own godhead, as they did love and wisdom and war and mischief. It was too strong a force in human affairs not to rate a divinity, after all.

I could feel my muscles unclench, the fatigues of the day loosen, as the music worked its familiar magic. Jared, Hamilton, Paul... they all spun away, powerless to disturb me. A cathedral of sound built over me, turning chaos into order, tenting the room with harmony.

The entry of the chorus broke my concentration. The singing seemed coarse and ragged compared to Rosa. The engineers hadn't been able to rescue those bass voices from the fogging of time. And then, my mind idling over this discovery, the Roman forum suddenly came into view. That tacky chorus in Druid drag, looking like fugitives from Hallowe'en on Christopher Street. I'd been right to leave early, right to hang on to my own high standards. Bellini massacred in Rome — it was an irony too awful to contemplate.

The cabaletta was almost finished now, Ponselle taking the high notes with ease, a celestial steeple-chase. This room, New York, the world, seemed a brighter place.

I shifted position, rolling over on my stomach. And then I saw it. So clearly it might have been at my side, in my hand. Vito's *gondolieri* shirt, the one I had washed in a fit of pique, of puritanism, scrubbing hopelessly at the kidney-shaped stain over the heart.

It was Vito's shirt that I had dropped on the bed when Anson Graef interrupted me in his bedroom. My skin chilled as I felt the goose-bumps rise. There was no doubt about it. The stain, kidney-shaped, was unmistakable — pasta, blood, whatever. Anson's face loomed before me, its sneer frozen into place. He thought I was snooping, prying into things that didn't concern me.

I sat up, deaf to the last of the music. *What was going on?*

And then, just as suddenly as it arrived, my panic abated. Of course Ellison had gone to see the Graefs after we got back from Europe. They'd be among the first people he visited. The shirt might have come into their possession in one of a dozen ways — a gift, a joke, a rag for use in painting or packing. My suspicions were out of control. I was turning into a paranoid asshole.

I got up, forcing myself to let go. Jared was right. I was headed for serious trouble. My head was a festering balloon. I put the record away, stripped and headed for a hot shower.

It was only later, much later, as I was lying rigidly waiting for sleep that a last ugly memory came to me. We'd been walking up West Broadway, the four of us — Ellison and Minnie in front, Anson and I just behind. Two handsome young gays, hardly more than high-school age, probably day-tripping in Soho as a relief from Staten Island or Westchester County, came toward us holding hands. I'd felt a rush of welcome at the sight — it was so sweet, so hopeful. Therefore it had been doubly disturbing to hear Anson Graef hiss under his breath and murmur an obscenity.

I had blotted it out — quickly, irretrievably — until now.

The man detested homosexuals. Was it possible that Ellison had misread him hopelessly — out of his own need?

Monday was cold and rainy, The kind of day that sends the October leaves into ugly scurries. I was due at Nino's at seven. In the meantime I had to get through the day. The students and I waltzed around each other, feinting and bobbing, looking for an opening. I realized, around 2 p.m., that the prizefight was turning into a war. I had to send two of my best students down to Rivkin's office. Two who had often hung around after school just to be with me.

Nino lived on East 110th Street, near the big vegetable market, in the heart of the barrio, the dark core of Spanish Harlem. After 96th Street the last of the Nordics left the car and I heard mostly Spanish, the hard words bouncing against the steel walls like pellets. Upstairs, on the street, quick curious glances followed me down the block. Two boys detached themselves from a group under a lamppost. I paused, letting them catch up with me before I turned down the deserted cross-street, but they just whistled and passed on. I would never know if I'd been paranoid or prudent.

The building Nino lived in was in better shape than those to either side. It looked as if the owner still lived in it. The door lock held firm until Nino's answering buzz admitted me. The sign on the elevator, in block letters, said DO NOT YOUSE. I climbed the four flights, noting that on the sixth step the slate tread had been completely worn so that a hole the size of a quarter showed. How many immigrant feet, I wondered, had it taken to wear through two inches of slate?

He opened the door wearing an apron tucked into his belt. He was in a buckskin shirt, jeans, boots. The bronze buckle on his belt was embossed with a rodeo rider. The whole outfit seemed hopelessly wrong. At the same time I felt a twinge of remorse. Nino had dressed like this, International Gay, to show that he belonged. That we were related. But I was here under false pretenses.

After he closed the door and reset the fox lock, he turned toward me. For a moment he seemed shy, speechless. His eyes danced around, as they had at the baths. He seemed to be look-ing for a place to hide. After a moment, though, he calmed down and came closer, turning his face upward for a kiss. He had to stand on tiptoe. His lips were crisp, his tongue burning. It darted quickly into my mouth and out again.

He took me around, holding my hand damply, showing me his treasures. I was able to get a better look at him. He was younger than I had thought, no more than thirty. Baldness had destroyed the first impression of youthfulness, but his face and neck were unlined, his forehead smooth. He was terribly proud of his possessions. He turned on the color TV for me, the Betamax, held up his Walkman. The electronic madness. I'd seen it before. In the parents of my students who built their homes around the TV and the new washer-dryer conbination. They had come to America so they could worship the new household gods.

The apartment was full of delicious odors. We were going to have osso buco, Nino told me, watching my face carefully for a reaction. I told him it was one of my favorite dishes. Not true.

He led me to the couch, still holding my hand, and reached for a photo album. It had been put there in advance, I was sure. He turned over the leaves and I saw fuzzy prints. A family group outside a stone barn. Nino at sixteen with lots of hair. Nino at twenty with a sauce cook's hat. He tapped his stubby forefinger on the dim faces under the acetate, telling me who they were. I didn't pay close attention until he said, "This my wife." I tried to focus on the blurry image. It must have been taken more recently; Nino's hair was more than half gone. He was standing slightly in front of a woman a little taller than he. Her black hair was coiled in a shining beehive over a long, aristocratic face. "Spanish. My wife Spanish." Nino looked around at me. "Barcelona," he said. The photo had been snapped at the foot of the Ramblas, under the statue of Columbus looking out to sea.

I leaned forward. "Where's your wife now?"

"With she's family." He shook his head. "Marriage no good. I no like." He reached for my hand and pressed it against the buckskin shirt. "I try. No good. I come here to this coan-tree. My family no like." His forehead was damp with the stress of finding words. His eyes grew rounder and sadder. "In America everything okay." He shrugged, as if he didn't really mean what he said. "I gotta good work." He pushed his chin forward and arched his eyebrows, a classic signal of skepticism. I knew what he meant. He squeezed my hand, still pressing it against his chest, and gave me a smile. Trust surged toward me. I tried to move my hand, feeling trapped. As trapped in his home movie as I had been in Avery's. But he held on.

"In Italia, they no understand," he continues. "Lotta bad name. *Uomina*. Men who are woman. You understand?"

I nodded. There were bad names everywhere.

"Before I come, I like Americans. Now I no like so much.

Nobody much nice. Have good time, goodbye. You different. You want to be my frain. You ask me."

I finally got my hand away. It was damp — from his sweat and mine. It was true. I had asked him. My remorse quickened into guilt. "Where do you meet these. . . Americans?" I asked. "At the baths?"

He shook his head fiercely. "All places. On street. Bars. Yais, I go bars sometime." He watched me carefully. "Americans fulla shit," he said calmly.

I felt suddenly drained. What had he expected to find? Sidewalks paved with glittering boys? I started to express some of this, but he interrupted me. "Osso buco, you like now?" He looked at me worriedly, then dropped his eyes in shyness. "Maybe. . ." he pointed in the direction of the bedroom. "First?"

"Let's wait," I said. And then, more lightly, trying to disguise the falseness in my tone, "How about a drink?"

He jumped up and went in the kitchen, returning with a liter of Soave and two glasses. It had been opened already, the cork just tapped in. As he poured, I said, "Nino, I want to tell you a story. About a friend and me."

He turned quickly. "You tell me you no gotta frain."

"I don't. But I want to tell you the story."

He listened, perched on the edge of the sofa, his head cocked to one side. He looked like a stuffed owl. His round eyes stayed on my face, all the way through the story of how and where I met Ellison, the years of friendship, the murder. From time to time he nodded to himself in a tired, fatalistic kind of way. He seemed to be moving away from the sound of my voice, shrinking inside his alien outfit. At one point his hand went to the photo album, as if it could give him nourishment. But when I came to the plastic sleeve, his body jerked and his eyes popped.

"Plastic?" He pointed to himself, then to me.

"Yes."

"*Che cosa!*" His voice was shrill, unpleasant. English seemed to fail him entirely then he continued in Italian. I sat quietly.

When he finished, I said, "I can still be your friend, Nino." I meant it.

He picked up the album and slammed it down on the table. It went off like a rifle shot. "I no understand!" he shouted. "I no understand this fucking coan-tree. America fulla shit!" His jugular stood out like a drainpipe. "FULLA SHIT!"

he shouted. "I go home. Soon!" he tapped himself on the chest. "You no like me. You no like me! You fulla shit too!"

He arched his neck and spat viciously on the floor. Another idea seemed to take possession of him. He stood up, his face ruddy with blood. "You think I killa your frain? Huh? You tella me, Mr. American boy, you think I killa your frain?" His voice broke. He looked around the room. I stood up, keeping the door behind me.

"No, Nino." I kept my voice low. "I think you can help me. That's why I came here."

"I no help you!" His face contorted and for a moment I thought he was going to cry. But just as quickly his features relaxed and his eyes narrowed shrewdly. "What you want?"

"I want to know who told you about the plastic."

A thin smile appeared. He jerked his head upward. "I tell you, what you give me?"

"What do you want?"

He laughed moistly. "What you think I want, Mr. American boy?" He put out his hand in the time-honored way, rubbing his thumb and forefinger. His eyes were dark moons. I thought I could read pain in them, behind the meanness, but I wasn't sure.

"I. . . I don't have much with me."

"How much you got?"

"A few dollars."

"You show me."

I took out my wallet. Two tens and two fives. I held it away from him. "The name first." He merely grinned, waiting. He might have been a peasant selling the first vegetables of spring. I took out the bills and handed them over.

"You know what I do with this" He folded the money into halves and balled his fist. "I go back Livorno with this. Yais. And somebody ask me. . . what happen in America. . . I say. . . America change. No like before. America fulla. . ." he spat out the word ". . . *shit*."

There was nothing more to say. I waited. Gradually his chest stopped heaving. He wiped his mouth and turned away. "Up," he said at last, motioning to the ceiling, "one floor. You find red door. My friend Troy. He give me."

Suddenly, stupidly, I thought about the osso buco. Food mixed with hope, love. A terrible feeling of waste came over me. I turned at the door to find him staring at me. His eyes seemed endlessly deep.

He motioned savagely for me to leave but I stayed one

moment more, trying to convey something across the gap. Regrets, apologies. And something else. Respect. Behind all the theatrics there was something that deserved my respect. I didn't care to name it, but I knew what it was.

I went out, repressing the urge to run downstairs and into the street. Inside, in some flabby part of me, I was hoping Nino had lied and I would be rid of the whole thing. The guilt and the promise and the burden. But he wasn't lying. The red door was there, one flight up. The namecard read *Troy Prentiss III*. I had no choice.

After my second knock I heard a dragging sound, as if a sack were being pulled across the floor.

"Who is it?" The voice was gnarled with suspicion.

"A friend of Nino's downstairs."

"Can't talk now. Sick. Come back later."

"When?"

"I don't know. Tomorrow."

"What time?"

He muttered something and dragged off.

It was dark on the street, and I hurried along, checking the alleyways and basement entrances. The vague menace of the neighborhood matched the feeling in my chest. It had been an ugly evening and most of it had been my fault.

The subway roared downtown. It was the hour when the night people were coming out of their caves and covens, changing the city from hardworking grub to insane butterfly. A black man in a white turban and jumpsuit stood in the center of my car and serenaded us with his saxophone — the hoarse, fruity tones bouncing around the interior. At last a transit cop came through and made him stop.

I saw the bit of graffiti as I was standing at the door, waiting to get off. Slate-green paint incised with a knife so the jagged letters showed bright and shiny.

FUCK

TO BE CONTINUED

The words slammed into my mind. There was only one way to wipe out this evening. One way with one person. I called him as soon as I got home. He was as cool and unflappable as ever, his voice free of surprise or — what would have been worse — triumph. As if he didn't bear the usual load of mischief, the load that plagued the rest of us. Maybe he just didn't have time. We made a date for the next day.

I slept like a child all night, dreaming of green fields and swaying long-stemmed iris. It was the best night I'd had in weeks and it lasted until the garbage trucks came through like giant devouring locusts, clanging me into wakefulness with the morning sun.

VIII. Troy

It was one of those rare October days, a bright banner of blue and gold unfurling over the city, making a promise that might even be kept. I suffered from bursts of elation all morning. They swept over me from nowhere, sending my heart into loops while I bagged the laundry, starting a low hum in my mind as I sorted Ellison's records at last. But it wasn't glands or biology or even the weather. It was something our cleaning lady used to call — on the high and windy plains of Troy, New York — happy fits. "Oh-oh, I can see it, you havin' an attack of the happy fits. Just keep outa my way, please, I got *work* to do." And she'd look mad and stalk off, leaving me more delirious than ever.

I left home an hour ahead of time and walked the streets of the Village, now choked with people drawn out of their homes for the Columbus holiday. It was a grand diverse crew. I took in the high spots. Young Italians with the pouty beauty of minor gods by Caravaggio. Black women with cotton-candy Afros, full of grace and guile. Latins in black chinos, legs like stilettos. Irish women with emerald eyes and sea-swept complexions. Jews like dark delicate hawks. The neighborhood seemed like a cross-section of the globe, a small parliament of human kind.

At last I turned west toward the river and the Morton Street pier, also known as Fire Island West. It was a long wooden finger jutting into the garbage-strewn waters of the Hudson. At first I couldn't figure why Avery had picked it for an afternoon's filming. It was filled with sunbathers, mostly male, pointed toward the last sun of the season.

It took Avery a while to notice me. He reared back from

the viewfinder, blinking his eyes to get the ache out. His glance swept casually across the watchers — we were three deep all around — but I knew what he was looking for. "Here, here!" I wanted to shout, but I only stood patiently, secretly, waiting for him to pick me out. And he did. His glance stopped, the spotlight of his face focused on me and he said, "Hi, Cord." Smooth and easy, even though there were fifty people around. It felt as if we'd just met in his studio, the two of us.

He'd picked the pier because the models he was filming — mostly young women — were modeling nautical outfits. Cruisewear, beach stuff, blazers. The big training ship docked permanently along one side of the pier — a relic of the Good War and the Maritime Trades High School — was called the *John W. Brown*. Avery was moving his models around the hawsers, bulkheads, up the gangway, spotting the angles, getting them to do their fine, careless model's walk while the camera ground. He worked without dolly or crane. Just a tripod for stationery shots. I could see his tall body take the weight of the camera as if it were a toy.

His assistant was dressed just as he was — in safari jacket, khaki pants, Timberland boots. I wondered who he was, how long they'd worked together.

I watched almost an hour while they moved the mannequins around. At last Avery flapped down the eyepiece and shouted, "That's it, kids!" Some of the female models clustered around him, resting their hands on his shoulders. They seemed faint and exotic to me — delicate creatures with hollow bones. I remembered Avery's goldfinches. Maybe he had a way with bird-like creatures.

He came over, red fans of color sprouting on his cheeks. "I want you to meet Kermit," he said. He waved at his assistant and Kermit strolled over. He was stocky, with fair skin and fine chestnut hair. He wore square glasses with gold frames. He took my hand energetically, but seemed to view me with a mixture of friendliness and distrust. I figured he'd heard the story of my flare-up about the taping.

"How about a beer? After we put the girls in a cab?" Avery was out of breath.

"Fine," I replied.

"Meet you at Kelly's across the way in ten minutes," he said. "Kermit and I gotta put the equipment away."

I strolled slowly down the pier to the bar on West Street. It was dark inside; all the fittings seemed to belong to the last century. Two men in motorcycle outfits were shooting pool. I ordered a beer and stood by the window, watching. I could see Avery giving orders.

He came in alone a few minutes later. We traded a long look. I could almost feel myself soaking into his meditative brown eyes. "I decided to let Kermit pack up." I had the impression — flattering, no doubt — that he wanted a few minutes alone with me. He held his head very high. I'm tall but I had the feeling I had to look up to see him clearly.

"What can I get you?"

"Oh, a beer, I guess."

I went to the bar and ordered, then turned and watched him move to a table against the wall. Seeing him bounce there, as if he were walking on springs, made me want to laugh. The physical messages are the most powerful, after all. (Once I smelled my mother's scent — the only kind she ever used, gardenia-flavored — coming from a mink-clad matron at Rockefeller center; I followed her for blocks, my nose leading me on, my whole system suddenly soaked in the past, half-drowned in an unbearable nostalgia.) Avery's body-language was a message aimed at me, a micro-joke, a private hieroglyph only I could decipher. And the strangest part of it was — he would never know. Even if I explained it to him in detail, he would never know. It wasn't in his sense receptors, in the million tiny cells of his body, to know. Not really.

I brought the beers to the table. "Tired?"

He touched his forehead with his big square hand. I could see golden hairs glinting at the fleshy edge. "A little. It's hard work. All that." He nodded toward the pier.

I waited a moment, then said, "I don't know why I called you. I couldn't *not* do it, if that makes any sense."

"It does, yeah."

"Though I sure as hell tried."

"I figured."

I pretended to an exasperation I didn't feel. "How did you get under my skin so fast? I've never dug filmmakers. Self-centered monomaniacs." His eyes held me. I could see humor in their depths.

"I can focus on more than one thing at a time," he said.

An old memory stirred. It had to do with Ellison. "I have this funny feeling that together we make one person."

He shook his head. "Negative. You're there and I'm here. To each his own head."

"You sure?"

"I'm sure. I've done it the other way and it's no good. Doesn't leave you any room."

"You need much room?"

"I believe in room, yeah. Don't you?"

I thought about Ellison. I'd left him lots of room. "I don't know," I said finally. "Sometimes you rattle around if you have too much." I wondered if I should tell him about Ellison. I was sure he hadn't heard the whole story from Hamilton. It would have been easy to do it here in Kelly's lounging in the late afternoon sunshine. But for some reason there didn't seem to be a pressing need.

"It's harder with two guys." He was speaking slowly, a frown on his clear forehead. "You gotta be careful. One can mind-fuck the other. I've had that."

My curiosity must have showed because he went on. "Yeah. In LA, when I was going to school. Film school. I had to be home at a certain time. I had to be nice to his friends even though some of them were creeps. We always fucked when *he* wanted to. . ." His eyes glazed over. "I finally split. Came east. Couldn't take that bullshit any more."

"So you didn't come east just to get work?"

"That was part of it. Part of it was to get away from Cucu."

"From who?"

"Cucu. He was Cuban. His real name was Abelardo."

"Well, Latins are famous for not leaving much room."

He chuckled quietly. "He even wanted us to use the same deodorant stick. That grossed me out totally."

I watched him. So he wanted to be free. Free and not-free, like everybody else. I thought about his collection of tapes. I wondered if he'd made them with Cucu too. That reminded me.

I lifted the manila envelope from the floor and put it on the table. He focused on it without curiosity. I slid the yellow container out. Recognition came slowly, then he looked at me warily. "Is that what I think it is?"

I nodded.

"What do you want me to do with it?"

"Whatever it is you do. Book it at the Palace. Call Studio 54."

The wary look faded, replaced by a slow grin. Our corner seemed illuminated with light.

"You didn't see the weirdest part," I murmured. "The spine."

He lifted the container in his big hand and rotated it. He batted his eyes a few times. "That's cool," he muttered at last.

"Goddam right it is. I'm even doing your publicity for you." The thick lettering on the spine jumped across the table at me. CORDELL-AVERY. And the date.

"You really changed your mind, I guess." He seemed to be seeing me anew.

"You knew all along I would."

"Negative. But I think it's great that you did." He paused. "Cordell McGreevy, film freak," he murmured. "Beautiful inside and out."

Kermit threw the door wide, bringing in a square of blue sky. "We gotta get going," he announced without sitting down.

I was outraged. "Where?"

"We're cutting a nudie. Worked last night. We gotta keep pushing or we won't finish." He checked his watch. "It's four o'clock now. C'mon, Avery, haul ass."

I turned to Avery. "You mean you have to work all night?"

"They pay better if we cut it fast. We'll each make five hundred dollars if we finish by tomorrow night."

"Nudies make you sexy," Kermit announced to nobody in particular. The pool-players looked at him without interest. Avery kept his eyes fastened on me. "We'll be working at my place," he said.

Kermit settled his glasses on the bridge of his nose. "Very sexy," he said again.

I glanced at Kermit. What did he have in mind? Avery, for the first time since I'd known him, looked a little uncomfortable.

"I'll try to make it," I said. "I gotta go uptown around seven."

Avery got up. "We'll be waiting."

Kermit's glance flickered over me. He bit his lip. "Hot guy," he said.

They talked about camera angles all the way up Christopher Street, oblivious to my presence. We parted at Bleecker with the most casual of nods. But I stood at the corner, watching Avery's fine easy walk for a full minute before heading home.

The red door opened slightly on my fourth knock. The chain was still in place. A puffy face, veined with purple, with tiny suspicious blue eyes, peered at me.

"Friend of Nino's?"

I nodded. the door closed. When it opened again I was facing a big man in his late forties. He was wearing a cambray shirt and levis, his beefy shoulders bulging against the blue cloth. His hair was thick and curly, mostly gray, but with traces of lemon yellow. Dense gray hair vined upward from his chest to his throat. He gave the impression of strength gone soft. Or of a stuffed teddy bear that had been mistreated for years.

"I don't know why you're here but come ahead." He stood aside and I started through the kitchen toward the living room. He moved behind me, walking with a slight limp. I held myself in tightly. No mistakes this time. Wiggams and Nino were at my elbow leering slightly.

"Don't mind the mess. I'm just getting organized."

The living room, beyond the kitchen, was terribly cluttered. It looked like the central archive of some failed enterprise — an insurance company gone broke or a shipping line with all its boats sunk. A light bulb dangled over a desk piled high with papers. There was a basket full of empty bottles in the corner. They were all Don Q. "Settling my grandmother's estate. Been too busy too get to my desk and clear all that paper work. What's your name? Friend of Nino's, eh? Sweet little man. He's not happy in this country but then who is? Your name?"

His voice was light and high, with an undertone of petulance. The grievances were massed just out of sight.

"Cord McGreevy."

"H'mmm. Irish?" His little blue eyes scurried over my face.

"Scotch and Irish both."

"Ah, Scotch-Irish. Deadly apart, beautiful together, like sodium and chloride. Scotch-Irish, salt of the earth. My grandfather was a sea captain, sailed out of Rotterdam. I have all his sailing logs. They're here somewhere. When were you born?"

"April 29th."

He surveyed me again, his lower jaw working slowly like the mandible of some giant insect. It was covered with a light grey stubble. "Taurus. You don't look like a Taurus. Never mind. Let me see your hand. Come here."

I didn't move but he seemed to forget what he had asked. He held up his own hand. "Crippled by arthritis. Hardly move my fingers. Look." He wiggled the fat sausage fingers with difficulty. "No cure. Been to every medium in town. No good.

Thank God my jaws still work. Never shut up. You want a drink? Make a vegetable cocktail with every vitamin in the book. Celery, carrot, cucumber, spinach. I'll make you one. I have to drink it three times a day."

He stopped and blinked rapidly. He appeared confused, as if he had lost his place. "Nino sent you? I wonder what for. Sweet little man. Let me see your hand."

He lumbered to the sofa, clearing away several bundles of newspapers. "Older I get the less I need people and the more I need newspapers," he muttered.

He sat down and looked up at me. This time he didn't forget. I moved toward him reluctantly. "Come on, don't be afraid." He patted the cushion next to him. I sat down gingerly, trying to keep my distance, but the couch sagged and I started to slide downhill towards him. He reached for my hand, handling it impersonally, like a slab of beef. He traced the palm lines with his forefinger while he made moist clucking sounds.

"You have a Simian line. Very rare. Last time I saw that was the gatekeeper in the Forbidden City. Just before they closed it to foreigners. Sweet little man. Your head line and your heart line have fused. Means a strong conflict between your emotions and your intellect. You solve them through will power. Very rare for a Taurus. Do you have a drinking problem?" He turned and stared at me. The skin on his nose was pink and grainy. "Yes you are. Definitely. I knew it the minute you walked in. I'm psychic, you know. One of the last of the great psychics." He chuckled. "Don't believe me, I don't care."

I withdrew my hand and moved to the far edge of the couch. "I'm what?" I asked.

"What? You're what?" He appeared confused again.

"You said you knew something about me the minute you saw me."

"Of course I did. You're a Munchkin. One of the new Aquarians." He held up his hand at the expression on my face. "I was predicting the second age of Aquarius long before the hippies got on to it. It's written in the stars. The end of guilt and fear. The end of homodyke killer mothers. I was telling people twenty years ago that as soon as Jupiter was in the ascendant you'd be able to suck a dick whenever you felt like it." He chuckled again. "Anywhere. The oldest of the arts. Goes back to the sculptures at Khajuraho, back to classical Greece, to Homer. The first man to take a cock in his mouth was hunting antelope with a flint knife on the Serengeti Plain and he got horny and went down on his hunting partner. Most natural thing in the world. Two young Neanderthals making love when the world was new and the morning stars sang together and the sons of God shouted for joy."

He paused for breath and I thought of a finely tuned motor — a Rolls or a Maserati — running out of control. "Some people say cocksucking is childish. You're suppose to outgrow it. What nonsense. Growing up has been mostly discredited anyway. Look around you. I'll take adolescence any day. Silly dreams. Puppy love. If you can't be faithful to your youth, what've you got?"

He reached into his jeans and took out a smooth ochre stone. It was a smoky topaz, big and fine. He said he had bought it from a Berber boy at the crest of the high Atlas, where the road to Ouarzazate reaches the summer snow line. He rubbed it between his thumb and forefinger while he talked, his voice high and remote.

"Actually we were our way across North Africa. We were making a pilgrimage to Biskra. We wanted to see where Gide did it five times in one night and spent the rest of his life explaining it away. There wasn't anything there but white buildings glaring in the sun, tombs and goats. My God, the goats. Up in the trees, down in the wadis. Ideal place for a Capricorn. Unfortunately, I'm a Leo." The moist chuckle sounded again. "Here, rub this. It'll bring you luck."

He held up the smoky topaz. I touched it. Its skin was smooth as water.

"I lived in Puerto Rico for many years. Bought a place in Loiza Aldea, a hut with a palm roof in a mangrove swamp, not even sure I have clear title. You can't judge the Puerto Ricans by what you see around here. City's ruined them. One of my neighbors in the village is El Grande. The most powerful witch on the north shore. His real name is Don Eugenio. A handsome man with seventeen children. That's not unusual. They all have seventeen children. I was at his house one night and I saw a woman spit out live frogs. Don't smile. Three live white frogs jumped out of her mouth. They were the evil spirits that had been making her sick. Xavert, that's his oldest son, told me how he did it. He had her drink milk with fertilized frog eggs. A few weeks later the eggs hatch. Incubated right in her stomach. She turned off her digestive juices and vomited up live frogs." His hand carved a frog out of the air. "When she saw the frogs she was cured. It's spirit magic. Good as penicillin. That's why Don Eugenio is rich. Owns half the beachfront at Loiza Aldea."

He stopped and seemed surprised at finding me in the room. His eyes focused into twin blue beams. "You don't want to hear any of that nonsense, you've heard it all before." I looked at him in stupefaction. "I know you. Remember you well. We met in Seville in '69. At the little grogshop next to the bullring. El Córdobes was fighting. You were drinking Veterano out of an olivewood cup. No." He passed his hand in front of his eyes. "That was someone else. I have you mixed up with someone else. Your name is... don't tell me..."

"Cord McGreevy."

"That's right. Scotch-Irish. I remember. You didn't tell me why you came. Nino sent you."

"Yes. He told me you could help me."

His eyes narrowed. His face became closed, suspicious. "I'm poor. Don't forget that. Look at the way I live. You know what my rent is? Eighty-five dollars a month. That's all I can pay. I'm a poor man."

"I don't want money."

A little earthquake convulsed his frame. He belched. "Good." He reached to the floor and picked up a glass. It was full of yellow rum; its sickly sweetish odor reached me. He sipped it, looking over the rim at me.

"I'm trying to trace the source of this." I took the plastic sleeve from my pocket. "A friend of mine was in the habit of using it. It's very important for me to find out where he heard about it."

He looked at the sleeve, his jaw grinding slowly. His breathing was heavy and strained. "The plastic cocksucker," he said.

"You've seen it before?"

"Sure. I told Nino about it."

"Could you... would you tell me where you came across it the first time?"

A gleam of cunning came into his eyes. "Cord McGreevy," he said. He began to laugh silently, a slow chortle that jiggled his whole body. He threw back his head and squeezed his eyes shut, repeating my name.

"What's so funny?" I could feel my anger rising.

He opened one eye, then the other, wiping away the wet from the corners with a fat freckled hand. "Don't pay any attention," he muttered. "You've never been to Argos, have you?"

"Where?"

"Argos." He shook his head, a jolly Buddha. "Never mind." I sat very still, thinking that any sudden move would disturb him more. Send him into total incoherence. "Just a passing fancy."

I held up the plastic sleeve, dangling it, trying to distract him. "Would you mind telling me about this?"

His face straightened out. He leaned towards me. The odor of rum was stifling. I reared back.

"How strong are you?" His eyes tunneled into me. I tensed, preparing to spring up. But he beat me to it. Suddenly he was on his feet facing me, his knees bent, his arms barred out. A wrestler's stance. He was strangely light on his feet.

"Come on, Cord, let's see how strong you are!"

He shifted position, moving his weight from leg to leg, still in his wrestler's crouch, his beefy arms out. "You were never scared of me before," he said, "and now I'm an old man."

I moved slowly, edging sideways off the couch. His breathing was becoming more labored, like a bellows. With a furious snort he charged me, grabbing low around the knees and tossing me back on the couch. His weight was mountainous. And suddenly I was angry. Angry and sick, mostly at myself for getting into this. I cursed and snaked my arm around his neck, my fist under his fat chin, and pulled up as hard as I could. The folds of his flesh gave way as my knuckles ground in, then I heard the hwee-hwee-hwee of a scraped windpipe. He was heavy but mushy and slack. I squirmed out from underneath and clamped his face, pinching his nostrils in a pressure hold. I kneed him quickly in the abdomen. The breath poured out of his mouth in a putrid wave. In another moment he was spread out, half on the couch, half on the floor, and I was on top, a knee dug into the hollow of each fleshy shoulder. I could have strangled him, and for one insane moment I thought I might.

"Get off," he whispered.

"You bastard."

He looked up at me and I caught the ghost of satisfaction in his eyes. "Get. . . off," he wheezed. He started blowing like a whale in distress. Horrible rattling noises came from his throat. Disgusted, I lifted one knee, then the other and stood up. I was a mess — shirt ripped, buttons gone, pants snagged. He got up very slowly, holding on to the couch, grunting and grasping, then lumbered slowly into the kitchen. He threw back his head at one point and I thought he was trying to get his breath. But when I saw his shoulders jiggle, I realized he was laughing. Laughing with satisfaction.

He turned around in the door of the kitchen and said, "Stay right there. I'll tell you all about it." He nodded. "The plastic cocksucker. That's what you want to know, isn't it?"

I stood undecided in the center of the room.

"I found out about it in Morocco," his voice was calm and matter-of-fact. He went to the sink and splashed some water on his face. He seemed almost dignified. "At the Casa Manolo. A famous male whorehouse on the Rue Dar el Baroud in Tangier. You know it of course." He wiped off his face and came slowly back to the living room. There wasn't a trace of embarrassment in his manner. We might have spent the last five minutes sipping tea. "Run by a Spanish queen named Manolo and his assistant. Hungarian, I think. Robert. Sweet little man. It's not really a whorehouse. It's a *maison de passe.* A place for assignations. Usually between five and seven in the afternoon. Everything happens between five and seven in the Arab world. Before that they're pretending to work and after that they're swilling rice or beating their wives. Those two hours are for boys. Ever make love to an Arab boy? Pick the flowers in the garden of Allah? If you haven't, you must. You don't know what you're missing."

He hunkered down and picked up his glass of rum. Miraculously, it was unspilled.

"Somebody's going to rewrite Genesis one of these days. Adam made love to his garden boy in the toolshed and for that he was thrown out of Paradise. That's the real meaning of the serpent story. I mean, why should God make a woman out of a rib when he could supply a fresh young boy instead? Adam's rib was an Arab nymphet with big dark eyes and a shlong down to his knees and if the Bible doesn't say so it's because Moses didn't want his mother to find out. Sit down, sit down."

When I didn't move he shrugged and lowered himself into a carved Spanish chair. He raised his head and gave me a beatific smile. He looked like an aging choir boy. "Yes, the plastic cocksucker. I founded out about it in the Casa Manolo. You see, the house has a special refinement. The rooms on the first floor have one-way mirrors. If you're not in the mood for performing yourself, you can watch. One day a very handsome man came in and chose Rachid. Rachid, my favorite. He spent his afternoons there, begging Robert for Coca-colas. I can't tell you how he loved Coca-colas. A fatal addiction. . . . Anyway, I

107

happened to be in the waiting room when they met. *Le salon gris.* I don't remember why I was there, but it doesn't matter. I saw them make their arrangement and I said to myself, why not? So I gave Manolo twenty dirhams, which was just half the usual fee and he uncovered two peepholes for me."

With a shudder I remembered the spy-hole at the baths. It seemed to be a world-wide affliction.

"The rooms are very bare. A mattress with straw in it, a basin and ewer. They kissed beautifully. The man, I could see, was starved. He had that special hunger northerners discover when they get to the Mediterranean — permission to let themselves bathe in all that lust. Millenia of lust. You've read St. Augustine, of course."

He looked up at me mischievously, raising the glass to his lips. I didn't reply.

"Anyway, Rachid took off his clothes while they were kissing. An athletic boy. He's all gold, hairless, with an ass like two Edam cheeses. I thought the man would do the usual. He didn't. He took out the little piece of plastic. Just like yours. Rachid didn't like it. He tried to wriggle away. Thought it was some kind of machine that would dissolve his middle finger." He chuckled at the memory. "He even jumped out of bed and demanded more money. But after he tried it he liked it. Everybody likes it. Wants more. That's its special charm, don't you think?"

He looked at me in a cunning way. Waiting for a confession, no doubt. "Who was this... this customer?"

"A professor. He had an interesting theory about promiscuity. Want to hear it?"

"No."

I might not have spoken. He sipped his drink and continued.

"The Greeks knew it was better with a stranger in the dark. What do you think that Psyche and Cupid business was all about? She didn't know who was screwing her but it was the best she ever got. After she held up the light and saw her lover was a beautiful young man with tiny wings growing out of his shoulders, it was never quite as good. They probably split up. Cupid found somebody who didn't hold up candles, who didn't want to know anything except he could fuck like a god. Don't you see? The Greeks were trying to tell us it's better in the dark with someone you don't know.

"This man, the one who told you that. Do you know his name?"

I waited, holding my breath. The moment, long-delayed, had arrived.

"Klaus Eckerman. German. Lives in Munich."

I felt a slow seeping of energy, as if someone had let the air out of my system. Munich. An ocean away.

He was smiling mischievously again. "You're in luck. I got a card from him just a few weeks ago." It took him three or four minutes, rummaging around in the debris on the desk. "Here it is." He held it out. It was a picture postcard. The Englischer Garten. On the back a cramped script. I couldn't make it out.

"He should be in New York soon. Try the Hilton in — let me see — about the middle of the week. And keep the card. A letter of introduction."

His face clouded over. His fund of goodwill seemed exhausted. He looked into his drink, swirling the viscous yellow liquid, then drained the glass at a gulp. When he spoke again, his voice was high and petulant. A wounded sound. "I used to be beautiful like you. Everybody after me. Taking me here, taking me there. That's all over now. Better to be a young June bug than an old bird-of-paradise. Mark Twain was right."

I started for the kitchen, the picture postcard in my hand. He sat very still, glaring at me, his lower jaw chewing over old grievances.

"Don't thank me!" he shrilled. "Nino said you wouldn't"

I stopped. So he had known all along. I turned to look at him, still cupped in the wooden arms of the Spanish chair. The light had gone out of his eyes and his jaw seemed sunken. He looked grey and sad — a toothless relic sitting in the mausoleum of whatever civilization he belonged to. He must have seen the pity in my face because he suddenly drew himself up, chunky and proud, and threw me a look of defiance. It was true — he must have been very handsome once. Inside the grossness and flesh there was someone else, someone clean and spare and fine. A line drawing, blurred by time.

"The poet Pindar," he intoned slowly, his eyes fixed on empty space, blue and unseeing, "died at the age of seventy-nine in his lover's arms at the gymnasium in Argos."

I stepped slowly into the kitchen. The words followed me, high and remote.

"They had been wrestling. Yes, wrestling. He died with one shoulder pinned to the earth, to the hard beaten earth of the palaestra."

My hand was on the doorknob. I opened the door slowly,

the words moving over my shoulder and into the dark hall.

"His heart stopped. But he died in bliss."

Gently I brought the door to.

"His lover wept. The whole world wept. But he died in bliss."

Two floors down I heard the rattle of chains and bolts as they swung into place behind the red door.

Avery met me at the door. I pressed him to me hard, bathing in the intimacy, the reassurance. He held me tight, searching out the reason in my face, but asked nothing. I knew he wouldn't. Not having to explain was the best part.

He looked at my torn shirt, my general dishevelment, but made no comment. The events of the last hour seemed absurd, surreal, in this apartment. There was no point in describing them. I suddenly remembered that Avery knew nothing about Ellison. I had kept them separate — past and present. Why was that? It was a question I would have to address soon. But not now. Not yet.

Kermit was sitting on the couch rolling some joints. He looked at me carefully. I thought I detected a faint hostility, as before, then dismissed the idea. I was still keyed-up from my encounter, still reading wrong signals.

"Smoke much?" It was a harmless question, but I didn't reply — just shook my head vaguely.

"We have a standing order. We can be paid off in grass instead of dollars any time a client wants."

I moved to the peacock chair and sank into it wearily. Avery had disappeared into the bedroom/workroom. I heard the clicking of his editing machine. Kermit laid the third joint next to the others, three neat white spikes. "This is great stuff." He pushed his glasses back on his nose. "We work better if we're a little stoned. You should have seen us just now. We intercut a fuck scene with a rocket blast-off. It'll blow your mind."

I seemed to be getting my bearings at last. Kermit struck me now as mild and unthreatening. What was I worried about?

"How long you been working with Avery?"

"About a year. We were at UCLA before that."

"You came east with him?"

"No. We ran into each other at a party."

"And you decided to team up."

He looked at me sharply. My nosiness hd gotten to him. "We decided to hang out together while we wait for the studio to send us a stretch limousine and an invitation to the première." He laughed suddenly, good-naturedly, and stuck out his legs. "Hell, Cord, we're not into a heavy sex thing if that's what you're worried about."

I tried not to let my relief show. "I wasn't sure..." I shrugged.

"Now you are," he said curtly.

Avery came in just then and stood watching us. "Break time?"

"We got company." Kermit nodded at me. They looked at each other. I thought I read several things in that look — curiosity, tension, jealousy. I stood up.

"Where you goin'?" It was Kermit.

"I don't want to interrupt."

For answer, Avery glided over and put his arms around me. "We've been waiting for you all night," he whispered. I looked into his eyes. I saw a flicker of amusement there. "I screened our tape for Kermit. He thinks you're terrific."

I stiffened. "You screened...."

His eyes didn't leave my face. "You said it was okay."

My words of the afternoon echoed in my ears. *Book it at the Palace, call Studio 54.*

"He's ready," Avery said, studying me. I smiled and relaxed. He knew me before I knew myself.

The first joint was lit and passed around. I sat in the peacock chair. Avery sat on the floor, resting his head against my thigh. I dug my hand into the massed curls of his hair. Kermit had picked up a magazine and was leafing through it.

The first change came easily, without a jolt, toward the end of the stick. The perpendiculars of the room sharpened and deepened. Then the angles sank back, into the depths of their angleness. I checked out a line in the ceiling. It was getting cleaner and darker. Then it turned into an abyss.

"How about it?" Avery addressed no one in particular.

He rose to his feet and turned to face me. He started to strip off his clothes. I concentrated on the movement of his arms, the sudden breathtaking appearance of honeyed skin and dark body hair. Kermit — wherever he was — didn't belong to this moment. At last he was nude. The perfection of his body imprisoned me. I could hardly breathe. He held out both hands and lifted me from the peacock chair. He began to unbutton my shirt. I threw back my head and started to laugh.

Suddenly I was aware of someone behind me. I registered the silken brush of pubic hair against my buttocks, the firm protuberance of something probing deeper. A pair of hands slid around and fastened on my nipples.

"Easy, baby," Avery whispered, sliding my shorts down. "Easy."

Let go, I thought, let go. I could feel Avery's brown eyes on me, sifting what he saw, trying to reach bottom. Suddenly, absurdly, I remembered seeing my mother once through the open door of the bathroom. I must have been about eleven. She had just gotten out of the bath. I saw her heavy ivory breasts, the soft swollen thighs, the patch of dark hair. I had soaked her in for an endless moment, until she saw me, gasped and covered herself with a towel. Then she closed the bathroom door.

The closing of the door! It had been the closing that closed everything. And now all that was changing, unshutting itself, resolving into openness. . . .

I seemed to be bathed in warm, moist air.

I turned slowly, arms out. They glided in on either side, pressing against me. I could feel Kermit's tight chest and his arm like a warm heavy bar on my waist. I put my own arm around Avery's back and registered the gentle slope of his spine. As if by a signal, they leaned their heads against me and the three of us stood silently, lambent statues in the center of the room. It felt as if some vital force were being transferred, skin on skin, bone on bone, in a round-robin of power and love. Suddenly Kermit bent down and a glowing stick appeared in front of my lips. I inhaled, hissing in air. Steam swirled upward. I don't remember how long we stood like that, passing the joint. At some point we unlocked and Avery moved off. I heard it, a miniature noise filled with meaning. I knew what he was doing. Part of me knew. Part of me said I was a liar. But when he came back I was ready.

"Cord." The voice was pure energy. "You know what I did?"

I nodded. "I know, baby."

"And you don't mind."

Big eyes searching my face. Vapors swirling upward. Doors opening.

"I don't mind."

"Okay."

I eased backward onto the couch as the ceiling spots came on. Kermit was on my lap, face down, his strong ridged back under my hands. Nice, dreamy, creamy. Feeling the skin and muscle of Kermit's bulgy back, the gold hairs glinting at the neck. The divine line, the centerfold, down the middle. I sighted along it. I could have shot a pellet to Mars. Bending down, smoothing my tongue down that gully. To where it deepened. Kermit shivering and squirming.

The third joint smoked in the center of the room. Our positions changing, a supple frieze of mouth and lip, hand and thigh, nipple and groin. The hard light of the two spots bathing us with noon sunshine. The whirring of the camera very distant.

Time seemed to condense into two presences, two events. The Avery event and the Kermit event. They were different. But how? The Avery event was taller. The Kermit event was heavier. Now they were coming at me, looking for a point of entry, trying to beat their way in... A cry and I was on top, clasping, rending, chewing... spilling to the floor, tasting the rubbery toughness of the flesh. *It could all be engorged, all taken in!* Cries, shrill, pleading, but it didn't matter. Nothing mattered except tearing at that luscious meat, making it mine, mine, divinely forever....

I was on my back. Something had happened. I had been pried loose. In my mouth something sweet and hard like candy. Suck the sweetness and the hardness out. Down below, out of sight, a pressure at my groin, pleasure engulfing me. A metal cannister pressing to my nostrils. Smell of hospitals, medicines. Something riding in me as the sweetness in my mouth increases, then fountains bubbling higher and higher and I am rising, levitating, wheeling through endless dim reaches of space, cresting on starfoam, tumbling in winds, and the sweetness is cascading in my mouth as my own body gives up its spirit-matter... and the tears make my eyes sticky and wet as I know that I am reborn in the death of the instant....

Doors opening, vapors swirling, all things visible at last.

Later, much later, lying in bed in the dark, Avery pressed sleeping against me. Kermit gone and the apartment settling down for the night. My head full of a strange clarity, a new knowing. Miscellaneous things that had tumbled about for years like cannon loose on a quarterdeck suddenly settling into place.

Ellison! Someone who was half-me, half-mine. *Let your body do the talkin'.* He had said that once. When? I couldn't find it now, under the overlay of the years. *I heard of the zip-less fuck but you're the fuckless zip.* He'd said that too, some other time, some other place.

Ellison angry at the world, taking his fury out on hotel clerks, bellboys, students, Vito. He had accepted me. A precious friendship. It hadn't been enough! The knowledge swept through me in a nauseating tide. It hadn't been enough! Second-best, that's all it was, second-best, ever and always the enemy of the best!

It must never happen again. Not here. Not with Avery. Not with anyone — ever.

And the Gemini thing. Was Ellison my truer self, the loving person I had glimpsed and avoided in the mirrors of my growing-up?

No! I sat up, sweating into the dark. Ellison was Ellison and Cordell was Cordell. Metaphor — the last indignity — would not be added to all the others.

And then, for the last time, the magnitude of my loss hit me. I turned toward Avery, a dark mass next to me, and embraced him. He barely stirred but I shook him until he woke up. "Ellison!" I cried into his warm arms, "Ellison!" I went on and on, repeating the name, until at last he covered my mouth with his big hand and rocked me into sleep.

IX. Klaus

The students noticed the change in me almost immediately.
"Mr. McGreevy isn't mad any more," I heard Elisa Gomez say.
The classes seemed to settle down, as if we'd been away for a
long time but now were home. On Wednesday I thought I
heard Forest Murmurs over a nutty story about a drunken ele-
phant named Zenobia — but I wasn't positive. Maybe it was
just the orchestra tuning up.

Liz Garrity was the next to notice. "You're feeling better, I
can tell," she whispered in the hall between classes. "You got
rid of those shoes that were pinching." She squeezed her face
into a pinched foot. "Nice to have you back," she groaned.

Even our guidance counselor Wendy Melasky, who drove
me up the wall with her analyses of student problems ("A
reading disability like that is based on resistance to authority
figures, have you tried reading comic books in class?") — even
Wendy didn't bother me.

I'd been staying with Avery for the past few nights, leaving in the morning before he was awake, fixing my own breakfast on his two-burner stove, letting the birds out for a
morning walk while I ate. Sitting under the plants, drinking
coffee, was like living in a jungle, complete with birdsong. I
felt like Rima. Or Tarzan.

I found myself thinking in new ways, too. Perhaps it was
Avery's easy presence, his disregard of clock-time, the casual
way we fell into bed at odd times. But my mind didn't seem to
want to move from point to point in the usual sequence.
Instead, my thoughts seemed to spread outward in vague
waves from a center. Radially. I oozed over and around a subject, enveloping it like an amoeba, then plop! a leap to the

115

next subject, with no connection in between. It wasn't unpleasant, just different, as if something had shaken loose. I tried to explain it one evening.

"I can't go from A to B any more. There's no path. No connection. It doesn't seem to *follow*."

"What do you want to go from A to B for?"

"I dunno. Because they're there."

"Who put 'em there?"

"What kind of dumb remark is that? There are causes and effects in the world. Sequences and order."

"That's the kind of bullshit they handed you in school. Pentagon thinking. If you build missile X you'll get peace. That's why we got enough missiles to blow up the world ten thousand times. Also the Russians." He blew smoke toward the ceiling. "You're going to another kind of organization, that's all. A higher level."

"I feel kind of lost. I can't read."

It was true. The little squiggles of ink were perfectly clear but at the same time strangely inert. No little squiggle related very well to what went before or after. Instead of using class-time just for reading or writing, I found myself telling long stories about my childhood in Troy, New York. Mostly about my anti-social behavior during early adolescence. I don't think they saw anything wrong with vandalizing vacant houses or dropping rocks in auto gas tanks. Strictly small potatoes.

"You've stopped being a weenie."

"What in the name of God is a weenie?"

He shrugged. "Somebody who reads and studies all the time."

I struggled with the thought of never escaping into books, into the phosphorescence of the printed page. The future seemed very bleak. "If I don't read, what'll I do?"

"Look at pictures. Do like I do."

"That's the last thing I want."

He batted his eyes. "You're just scared of being blissed out. C'mere."

I moved to the couch where he was lying, a pillow under his neck. He was right. There were pictures that were worth a thousand words, and he was one of them.

I had playground duty next day — a chore I'd found diffi-cult this term. Ellison and I always arranged our schedules to do it together. We'd usually wind up more hoarse and sweaty than the kids — not from scolding them but from being caught up in their games. I'd been aloof this term — I couldn't help it

— but today, somehow, I got involved in touch football. Not just refereeing, playing. At one point, calling out signals, I was aware of Rivkin's white face at the second-story window. I could almost hear him. *You maintain order in the classroom by earning the respect of the students.* Well, I thought, as the ball snapped to me, this was no way to earn it, but it was an awful lot of fun.

Johnny Lombroso had just kicked to our side when I saw him. I didn't make the connection at first — it was altogether too strange — but when the ball hit my shoulder and my team screamed in frustration at my carelessness, I found it. Anson Graef, in a shapeless overcoat, with a tweed golfing cap pulled low over his face, was standing across the street. He seemed to be scanning the school, top to bottom. I hadn't recognized him, partly due to the cap and partly because I didn't associate him with this side of town, this side of my life.

I was aware of hands tugging at me, trying to get my attention back to the game. But if Anson had come up to see me, was standing there not knowing how to locate me, I'd have to go over.

"You gonna play or ain'tcha?"

I was surrounded by a circle of small, aggrieved faces.

"I'm sorry, I gotta. . ."

Graef waved.

"You gotta what?"

He was not waving at me. I turned around. The windows of the school loomed blankly above. Another glance across the street showed me Graef standing in front of a coffee-shop, lighting a cigarette. I was in his direct line of vision. I didn't want him to see me.

"Mistah Muh-Greevy, what you *doin*?"

Querulousness turned to outrage as I stepped quickly behind a girder holding up the fire-escape. I'd loused up the game for good.

Just then the bell rang and the playground, with the usual delaying tactics, began to clear. I didn't have much time. My room would be in an uproar if I turned up too late. It was my slow-learner class, too.

He'd almost finished his cigarette, lipping it impatiently, turning in all directions, when she rounded the corner. She was carrying one of her big portfolios, the laces hanging loose. I heard her long, windy halloo as she crossed the street.

He gave her a peck on the cheek, then I watched her signal that *that* coffee-shop was no good. She motioned ahead and

117

they set off. I knew where they were going — to Broadway where there was a deli that made terrific pastrami sandwiches.

Where had Liz Garrity met Anson Graef? Why had neither he nor Minnie ever mentioned that they knew another teacher at my school?

The questions haunted me all afternoon.

After school that day I went down to my apartment. I hadn't been there in several days. There would be mail, messages on my machine. Also, clean clothes.

It was at my mail-box that my mind slipped back into the old groove. It was a picture postcard from Thorpe-Ferrara Interiors. Their shipment had arrived from France. A preview party for the trade and a few friends, at their shop on Madison Avenue. I turned the card over. It showed a porcelain relief — an oriental gentleman bowing from a nest of amber ferns. The caption read, "Details from the ceiling, room with chinoiseries, Royal Palace, Madrid." A phrase of Jared's recurred to me. *Give them the benefit of the doubt.* I had, so far.

After my apartment chores were done, I headed for the Jefferson Courthouse Library — a dizzy pile in the heart of the Village, designed by someone who hated straight lines. Liz hadn't lied. The QE2 was shown under *Shipping/Mails* as incoming on September 2. I went out to the lobby and called Cunard. After some canned instructions to wait, I was connected to Passenger Service. They said it was against policy to release passenger lists. But they did say that on that westbound crossing the ship had stopped first at Cherbourg, next day at Southampton — a double stop that only happened four times a year. I searched my memory. Had Hamilton said they'd boarded in Cherbourg? I remembered clearly that Liz had sailed out of Southampton.

Hanging up, my hand closed over the postcard in my pocket. Liz's friendly face was still in view. The two events became one. Why not invite Liz to the preview with me? Watch and wait. It was so simple really. I could have my own confirmation in living color.

I made the call to the Hilton on my way to Avery's. "This is Dr. Eckermann speaking." The voice was crisp, abrupt. "Ah, yes," he replied to my explanation, "a friend of my good friend Troy Prentiss. He thinks we have something in common, *ja!*" A pleased, strong German voice. "You will be free perhaps on Friday? Tonight and tomorrow I am in meetings, I am sorry. We will go someplace on Friday?"

Friday was the evening for Paul and Hamilton. I told him I would be busy until ten or so. "We will meet later," he said smoothly. I agreed. We made a date for the Hellhole — at his request. I was to ask the bartender to point him out. "I think we will be good friends, it is Cordell, *ja?* Until Friday. *Gutbye.*"

The final queston was how much to tell Liz. She only knew that I was "checking up" — as she put it. There was something unethical about using her as a plant, a cat's paw, in all of this. On the other hand, if she knew what I was up to, she might warn Hamilton and Paul in advance. I might not get the unrehearsed reaction I wanted.

Of course, she'd been a friend of Ellison's. If she thought all this was leading to the identification of his murderer, she'd undoubtedly be glad to help. Still, it would be simpler not to clue her in. I eased my conscience by deciding to ask her to dinner before the party.

That night I brought Avery up to date. I'd already told him about the plastic sleeve, showed it to him, filled him in on some details about my search. But I'd kept the doubt about Hamilton and Paul to myself. It seemed... well, unattractive.

He waited a long time after I laid out the facts. Finally I said, "They lied about their arrival time, don't you see? That's the puzzler in this whole thing."

His voice was flat when he spoke, as flat as I had ever heard it. It seemed drained of everything except gentleness. "You don't know the real story, Cord. There's no way those two guys could damage another human being." And then, as if echoing, he said, "Why don't you give 'em the benefit of the doubt?"

I thought about Liz. I hadn't told Avery about my plan for her. The cat's paw. Why? Because, I admitted grimly to myself, I knew what he would say.

The benefit of the doubt.

La Dame Blanche was one of those restaurants where they put the pastries on a little table in the center of the room and surround them with fresh flowers. It also had a maître d' who wanted to look and sound French but was unquestionably Greek. It didn't matter, though. The dinner had been superb.

Liz was looking madly chic. No trace of excess in her slimmed-down figure (black velvet pants-suit with big mother-of-pearl buttons gleaming like full moons, and God knows what else underneath, squeezing flesh). Her skin was lustrous and pale against the velvet, the shadow between her full breasts deepening to dove-grey. She closed her eyes blissfully as she put away the last of a créme caramel.

She'd accepted my invitation eagerly. I hadn't bumped into her for a week or so. The third floor, where the arts, crafts, music and shop studios were located, seemed to have a life apart from the rest of the school.

"Cordell, honey, nobody's asked me out for dinner for so long I'm not sure I know how to behave in public. Yes, I'd love to."

She looked tired. The term was only eight weeks old but it was beginning to tell on all of us.

I offered to pick her up — shades of my senior prom — but she demurred. "My place is a mess, I'll meet you somewhere." We arranged to meet in front of Bloomingdale's, not far from this restaurant.

She was ready to leave the faculty room when I asked. I tried to keep my voice casual but there was a catch in it anyway. "I didn't know you were a friend of Anson Graef."

She went through one of her sudden changes at that. Her eyes glimmered, her bosom swelled dangerously. The next instant she was her old fey self. "Do you know Anson? Why goodness me."

I didn't mention Ellison — don't ask me why. Just said I'd been introduced by some friends, had gone to a recent show in their loft.

She moved around the room as she replied. "Graef's Art Supply has saved me hundreds of dollars. Do you know what it costs to buy a tube of paint these days?" She paused. "Lots of people get to know Minnie and Anson. Their shop is to New York what the Delacroix studio used to be to Paris." She gave one of her whooping laughs at that and made me promise to walk her to the subway real soon.

All this flashed through my mind tonight as the waiter cleared the dishes and brought us demi-tasses, strong and aromatic. The next instant it was forgotten. Her eyes had widened as she peered over my shoulder. "Look, " she whispered stagily, "she's wearing the cold buffet."

I turned. A woman had just entered with a half-pheasant on her head. "It looks like the temple scene in *Samson and Delilah*," she said, "you know, where the priestesses come in dressed like game birds?"

"I never saw them come in like game birds."

"Then you haven't seen *my* production."

"No I haven't, lamebrain, and neither has anyone else."

She looked at me in shock. "The Hamburg Opera is bidding on it this very minute. They have all the sketches. I'm expecting a cable tomorrow at the latest."

I gave her a long intimidating look. "If you don't act your age I'm going to give you cabfare and send you back to North Dakota."

She glared at me. Her personality seemed to have hidden traps in it, bamboo deadfalls, where you might be impaled instantly. "What do you mean by that?"

"I . . . why, nothing. Just joking."

"That's not a joke. It's a deliberate insult."

"Come on, Liz, I'm not doubting your professional talents. I just haven't seen any of your designs."

"I have rafts of them at school You never even come upstairs to look."

"I mean onstage." I spread my hands apologetically. I was sorry I'd gotten into this.

"That doesn't mean a thing," she snapped. "Lots of people have seen them. People who know more about it than you do."

I mumbled something, trying to make amends. What was it that set her off? Just as abruptly she changed back.

"Besides," she pouted a little, "I'm from South Dakota. No one's from North Dakota except a few gophers."

"Okay, South Dakota." I reached across to touch her hand but she pulled it away. "When are you going to quit teaching those kids to draw funny pictures and set yourself up in a studio of your own?"

She liked that, her pixie look lighting her face. "As soon as I get the word from Hamburg."

I changed the subject. "You never told me where you studied."

She waved her hand, brushing the query off. "Oh, everywhere. Courses here and there. You know, wherever the good teachers are. I've gone to school in about five different places, from Santa Cruz to New Jersey." She wrinkled her nose. "Let's not talk about that. I'm having such a good time. Are you?"

I was, in spite of a small knot of anxiety in my stomach. My plans for the evening were balled up in my gut, making me tense. I had hardly gotten my money's worth out of the meal.

"You still all by your lonesome down in the Village?"

I managed a small smile. "All by my lonesome. I guess I like it that way."

"No you don't. You're just saying that." Her voice brought me up sharply. It occurred to me that life with Liz might be a running battle. The warlike pixie.

"Come on," I said abruptly, "we better get going." I signaled for the check.

"Now just a minute, don't rush me." She was suddenly the country girl again. She lifted her purse to the table and started rummaging in it. At last she found what she was looking for — a folded page from a sketch book. "Are they going to be surprised! I brought them a present. Hated to fold it, though."

She opened it and showed it to me. It was a watercolor, two runny figures with featureless faces and odd outfits.

"You know who that is?" I shook my head. "That's Aristotle and that's Homer. I sketched them the night they won the prize."

"You mean that's Hamilton and that's Paul?"

"Yep. Isn't it a hoot?"

"I'd never have guessed."

She took that as another insult. Her voice rose. "You don't know anything about costume design. What do you see from the balcony? You see color and you see shape." She smacked her fist on the sketch, now spread out on the table. "You can't bother with detail when you're designing for the theater! Look at the stuff Bakst did. Look at what Picasso did. *They* knew!"

I guess I looked suitably crushed, because she reached over and patted my hand. "Didn't mean to lecture you." She wrinkled her nose. "Just there's so many dummies around." She giggled again, her eyes sparkling. "Not you, Cordell, you're just uninformed."

I waited a moment, waited until the idea, born a moment ago, could gather strength. At last, I said, very lightly, "Date it."

"What for?"

"So you'll always know when you did it."

She bit her lower lip while she gazed at me. "That's not why you want me to do that."

"Okay, do it as a favor for me."

She turned her head to one side, then looked back quickly, as if she might catch me unaware. "All right, but I'll have to do it in lipstick. That's all I have."

122

"Lipstick's fine. September first."

She scribbled the date quickly, the letters lying on the page like red worms. When she finished I slid the paper away.

"It's *my* present, Cord!

"It's from both of us." I folded it and put it in my jacket pocket.

The dinner check was half my salary for the week.

The crowd at Thorpe-Ferrara, Interiors, was about what I expected. A few familiar faces — Jared, for one, who seemed to be barricaded behind a Coromandel screen by an excited woman in an oversized hood-collar — but mostly the usual middle-aged men in two-toned shirts and Guccis, single women toughened by years of living alone and a few mom-and-dad types who stood uneasily apart in this sea of professionals, smiling too much.

Hamilton was delighted to see Liz. When she stepped past the young man taking hats and coats, he seized her and flung his arms around her. He didn't see me just behind. "Guess who I came with," she said when he released her. I watched his eyes flit from her to me, but whatever I was expecting didn't happen. "Of course!" He smacked his hand to his forehead. "Why didn't I think of it? You both teach at the same school!"

"Yep," she whooped, "good old P.S. 9."

"Why didn't you tell me?"

"Why didn't you ask? Where's Paul? Where's the booze?"

I followed her in and we went through the same routine with Paul. His reaction was quieter, of course, and there was one moment when I thought I saw something flash in his eyes, a flicker that was gone before I could decipher it. I tried to recapture it as I worked my way toward the bar, but without success. It might have been no more than host's nerves.

I looked around for Liz after ordering a stinger. I had lost her already. Drink in hand, I started maneuvering toward the wall, out of harm's way. Paul and Hamilton, both in blue blazers and trousers in the Stewart plaid, were greeting more guests at the door. The party area looked very dramatic. Most of the furniture that usually cluttered the showroom had been moved out, leaving only a dozen handsome pieces displayed on small carpeted platforms around the room, their winy wood colors somber against the white walls. Most were French provincial pieces, heavy but charming. The landlady on the Ile du Levant had a good eye. Or her great-grandmother did. I wondered what Thorpe-Ferrara Interiors had paid for these heirlooms.

Jared had worked loose from the lady in the hood-collar.

"How are you?" His black-walnut eyes trained on me solicitously.

"Not good. Not bad."

"They've done a marvelous job with this place. How do you like the furniture?"

"Great."

"I wish I could afford that one." He nodded at an armoire in the corner, then turned to me. "Have you forgotten about. . . what you were telling me?"

I looked around nervously. "About Paul and Hamilton?" They were still at the door. He nodded. My hand brushed the sketch paper in my side pocket. "I. . . I haven't decided yet." I held up my hand. "Don't give me any good advice, please, Jared."

His eyelids flashed down, hooding his eyes. "I wasn't going to. You don't listen anyway."

I had an answer ready, but Liz walked up. I introduced her to Jared.

"You should see what they've got downstairs," she glowed, "enought stuff to restore Versailles."

"The basement?" I asked. "How'd you find it?"

"Hamilton took me."

"What did he have to say?"

She knew what I meant because she hesitated. "He said. . . maybe this is none of your business."

I looked at her hard. "Maybe it is."

"He asked me if you knew we came over on the QE2 together."

"What did you say?"

"I said sure."

"What was his reaction?"

"Nothing. Just kind of clammed up."

I turned to Jared, trying to keep the triumph out of my voice. "What do you think of that?"

"I don't think anything."

"What's going on, will someone let me in on the secret?" Liz's voice was shrill. "I hate all this mysterious business."

Jared turned toward her. His scars had begun to glow. "Nothing, except Cord thinks Hamilton and Paul had something to do with Ellison's death."

"Ellison?" she said, too loudly. Several people turned to look at us. "*Ellison?*"

I was furious at Jared. "I'm not saying they're connected. It's just the timing. They told me they were aboard ship until after Ellison died. But you told me you got here Saturday morning. That means they were here, then, at least a full day beforehand. Why did they lie? That's what bothers me. Why?"

"You don't know anything about it." Her voice was jarring. "You don't know *anything.*"

"Yeah, but I know a little more than anybody else, which is a lot."

"You puzzle me, Cord, you really do." It was Jared, his tone infuriatingly superior. I bridled.

"What is it? That I'm paranoid? Or guilt-ridden? I forget."

It was Liz who replied, her ample bosom rising and falling. "Well maybe you are! Why don't you put Ellison out of your mind?"

There it was again. It seemed there was a conspiracy to make me forget. I closed my eyes. Maybe I was paranoid. I felt suddenly, absurdly, unfriendly toward both of them.

When I opened my eyes, Hamilton was standing next to us. "Everybody okay here?" His glance rested on each of us.

With a feeling I was falling from a great height, I took out the sketch and handed it to him. "Here's a present for you," I said, "from Liz and me."

I heard a sudden intake of breath from Liz. Jared coughed. Hamilton unfolded the paper, looking puzzled. It took him a minute to make it out. "That's us!" His face creased with pleasure. "Homer and Aristotle!"

"Sure is," Liz was torn between pride and pain. "I did it the night you won."

"Wait'll I show it to Paul!"

"She dated it too." I motioned to the lipstick. It was smudged now, amost unreadable. "September the first. The night before you docked."

Hamilton bent his head to look at it. I could see the short grey hairs on the back of his neck. I was suddenly overcome with regret but I went ahead anyway. "The night before Ellison was killed."

He looked up quickly, his eyes darting from me to Liz and back again. We stood unmoving for a long moment, four figures in a frieze. I don't know what would have happened if the lady in the hood-collar hadn't bulldozed her way in and grabbed Hamilton by the arm.

"Hamilton," she shrilled, "I want to buy the commode. The marquetry is gorgeous! Simply gorgeous! But I won't pay your price. Come and haggle with me."

She pulled him out of our circle. His face, when he looked back, was dim and haggard.

"You bastard," Jared snarled.

"Yeah? Now I have proof!"

"Proof of what?"

I paused. "Proof that. . . ."

"Cord, are you all right?" It was Paul. Behind me. How long had he been there?"

I got out a strangled reassurance.

"Why don't you let Giorgio fix you another drink? You look like you've been working yourself to death." He came around. His eyes were dark, his face shiny and pale.

I shook my head, backing away. Suddenly I wanted out, out of the party, from all of them and from the tearing certainty in the back of my head.

I put down my drink and hurried toward the door, my name rolling across the room from Liz and Jared and Paul in tiny puffs of indignation. What did they expect me to do? Stand around and pretend that nothing had happened? That I hadn't been lied to? That my friendship with Hamilton and Paul, one of the finest things in my life, hadn't been abused?

As I groped my way out the door, down the four steps that led to Madison Avenue, the circuits in my brain flashed emergency signals. To whom should I be loyal? Ellison? Hamilton? Jared? Myself? Everyone wanted something different. It seemed that I, the accuser, was accused. Of what? Of being right? Didn't I have the right to be right?

I don't remember how long I walked, taking chances at the intersections, unable to stop. At last a phone booth at the corner of 49th signaled to me. I stopped and fished out a coin.

It took me a long time to punch out Avery's numbers, my head dizzy, my fingers cold. As the phone rang I rested my head against the aluminum sheathing. *Be home, be home.* Finally a robot voice broke its electronic silence and told me the party wasn't answering.

I was surrounded by the forlorn tinsel of Times Square when I remembered my date with Klaus Eckermann. He seemed remote, a figure from another landscape. The trail of the plastic sleeve — a wretched chase of hares and hounds through the forests of the night — was something that had led nowhere. I thought of Wiggams, Nino, Troy Prentiss. Marginal creatures, all eager to ensnare me. Would this one be any different?

I tried to recall Avery's schedule. Was tonight the fundraiser at Lincoln Center? The preview at the Film Forum? Was he with Kermit? And then, quite suddenly, Jared's question resounded in my ear. *Proof of what?* I had started to answer it, but had been interrupted. Did I really have the answer?

I stopped, amid the swarm on Broadway. I had proof of nothing except that Hamilton and Paul had been in town that night. Along with eight million other New Yorkers. I was nowhere near the end of my quest. In fact, I'd made no progress at all.

And then a familiar doggedness took over. I wouldn't let go. I wouldn't give up. Behind the lies, the warnings, the premature conclusions, there was something else to discover. About Ellison. About myself. About all of us. And what were the alternatives — Drosky and Buzzini?

I would keep my date at the Hellhole.

"You are Cordell, correct?" The man who greeted me in the bar area was short and strongly built, with ash blond hair and a fringe beard. He was in full leather regalia — brown, not black. He looked almost dapper among the black-clad legions in that room. His pants seemed to be bristling with zippers. I put his age at thirty-five.

As I identified myself and apologized for being late, he examined me approvingly. I'd changed clothes at home — out of the jacket and tie and into jeans and grey T-shirt. I'd checked my nylon jacket at the little booth in the rear; it wasn't part of the dress-code.

"I have been enjoying myself, I do not worry," he remarked, in accented English. He looked around the bar slowly, the fringe beard outlining his face with a dark brushstroke. His face had a flat medieval look; I might have seen it looking out of a Dürer miniature. "I come here always when I am in your country." He sipped his beer. "Germany has S&M but we are nothing compared to you. American technology always leads the way." *All-vays leets de vay.*

I started to say that our technology was superior but when Germans went in for S&M they did it on a national scale — then checked myself. I hardly knew the man.

"Tonight it is special here, we are lucky." When I looked surprised, he added, "The Department of Lower Education."

He smiled, showing strong, even teeth. "There is class tonight." He motioned to the corridor leading from the bar to the cavernous back rooms. I knew that area well — a dim warehouse where prowling men made contact.

"Of course, I like downstairs best." He showed his teeth again. The floor below, I knew, was where the real raunch went on, mostly around the bathtubs in the center room. "Downstairs in Nibelheim." He smiled again.

"Troy said you had some information for me." My voice sounded cold, almost snappish. I knew I'd made a tactical error from the way his eyes hooded down. When he looked at me again his expression was amused. I had walked into his trap. Now he would enjoy playing with me.

"Cordell." His tone was authoritative. "We will discuss that in a moment. I think I can help you. But first you will tell me why you want to know about this... this little plastic."

He waited. A few men drifted past us, beers in hand, on their way to the back. In the far corner of the bar I could see an older man in a Stetson kneading the nipples of a willowy youth. A fierce concentration had settled on the faces around me. They reminded me of hunting animals.

I began to talk, not telling the whole story — he would have gotten details from Troy anyway — just enough to transmit my need, my urgency. He kept his eyes on my face. When I finished he asked how Ellison had been killed.

"With a knife."

"With a knife." He mused over this for a moment. "Do the... ah, the police find the knife?"

"It wasn't recovered. But..." I stopped. I really didn't want to share any details with this man.

"You stop. Why is that, Cordell?"

"It was a dull knife. The edge of the wounds..." I took a deep breath, "...were torn, jagged. If it had been a sharp instrument the incision would have been cleaner."

His eyes glittered. "Surgeons use only the sharpest instruments, *ja*?" He paused, sipped his beer. "So. You tell me, please. This man was your lover?"

"Sort of."

"Sort of. I do not understand."

"We were lovers at first. After that we were friends. For a long time."

"Lover and after that friend. This is the homosexual way, *ja*?"

"Could be." I thought of other answers to that — Ellison's

for example, but said no more.

Eckermann nodded, then went to the bar and set down his beer. Glances followed him; he was a handsome man. He beckoned me over a little later. When I got there he was holding up a square of paper. I could see glee in the depths of his eyes. "I write here what you are looking for. A name, *ja*?" He smiled broadly. My anger at being teased was just what he wanted. "I give it to Peter," he continued, handing the slip to the bartender, "who is also the *Garderobenwärter*. What is your number please?"

I reached into my pocket, still seething. "Twelve."

"Twelve." He repeated it to Peter, who nodded, looking slightly embarrassed. "Peter will put it into the pocket of coat number twelve. When you leave, you will take it and read. But first, we will go to the back. Together." He moved off, stopped, waited. Peter still had the square of paper clutched in his hand. He'd no doubt been tipped well. I would have to make a scene or play the game. With the sickening feeling that I had been through all this one time too many I decided to play the game.

It took a while for my eyes to adjust to the gloom, punctuated here and there by circles of dim light. In the center of the first room, narrow wooden stairs led to the lower floor. There was a steady traffic up and down. Eckermann waited for me at the top. "We will save that for later," he whispered. His breath was sweet and mint-flavored.

Gradually I became aware of a strange shape hanging from a wooden frame against the wall. Long and lozenge-like, it swayed slightly as curious hands explored it. It was completely encased in wide black tape. I moved over for a better look. Encased in tape — but not completely. I could see genitals protruding.

"How do you say?" Eckermann had followed me. "Up over?"

"Upside down," I replied. "He's hanging upside down."

"He is excited by it, I think." Eckermann pointed toward the man's cock, which was far from flaccid.

I saw someone go up and give it a tweak. A moan of pleasure or pain sounded from the taped mouth below. A mingled sensation of excitement and fear coursed through me. Suddenly I was aware of Eckermann's hand on my back, moving down. "You find that interesting?"

I stepped away; his touch made my flesh crawl.

Another sight caught my eye — six pinpoints of light

reflected in the mirror over a counter. It was the bar, no longer used, across the room. On the counter a man wearing only a leather harness was stretched out. His hands and feet were being held down by two other men. On his chest and stomach six candles, anchored by their own dripped wax, were burning. The man groaned as more wax flowed onto his skin. He tried to twist away but was prevented. The men holding him were both bearded, impassive. They might have been assisting at a minor operation.

One of the candles was guttering, the flame almost at the skin. The victim's groans rose in pitch. The bearded men leaned more heavily. The man was almost shrieking now, his legs writhing. And then, with a sweep of the hand, one of his captors swept the guttering candle to the floor. I stepped on the flame and moved away.

I'd lost Eckermann for the time being. I glanced through the opening to the adjacent room. Around the alcove in the far corner a crowd had collected. I knew what that meant.

The man in the sling was young and well-muscled, the man bending over him middle-aged but slender. He was wearing steel-rimmed glasses. I jockeyed around for a better position. When I saw it my stomach skidded and my throat burned. The man above had his arm plunged in almost to the armpit! I'd seen fisting but never this. He rotated his arm, and then a shock of surprise and horror ran around the circle. The man had just removed his arm and we could see that it was cut off just below the elbow — in an accident, no doubt. The stump, tapered, would have easy entry to the sphincter. He'd pushed in no more than six or seven inches. The buried arm had been an illusion, an optical trick.

I moved off to find Eckermann standing raptly at the edge of the circle. He saw me and spoke. "That I have not seen before."

I thought about the supremacy of American technology but said nothing.

He studied me for a moment. "I think you are enjoying yourself, Cordell" I nodded grimly. I wasn't exactly bored.

"Well then, if you are not interested by electricity, we go downstairs." He signaled to a group in another corner. I could see wires going from a hand-held apparatus of some kind. The man holding them was looking for a taker.

"Downstairs," I echoed.

The usual activities were going on in the nearer tub. As usual, I found the smell of piss offensive — something to do with unclean latrines in foreign countries. I held my breath for a moment then, at Eckermann's nudge, moved toward the other tub. The Department of Lower Education had really come through on this one.

There were two men, both attractive. One was lying on his back in the tub, whose surface was glistening wetly. The other was standing beside the tub. A thin plastic tube, the thickness of a straw, ran from one cock to the other. It took me a long time — or was it seconds? — to figure it out. The men were connected by a catheter. The one lying in the tub was taking the other man's piss via gravity flow *up his own urethra*.

Eckermann, beside me, was laughing silently. At last he turned to me. "You understand why I come here every year?" His eyes were merry. "It is like a couturier who goes to Paris. I come to see the new collections."

Did I reply? I don't remember. I only know that I began to move away, heading toward the stairs. I'd had enough.

But Eckermann was right behind me, chuckling. When we got upstairs he took my arm. "Come, Cordell, in a few minutes you are free."

He pulled me toward the back, toward the sling. Somehow, without admitting it, I knew what was coming. Some others must have known too, because a small crowd followed us. The one-handed man was there, waiting.

Klaus pulled at his zippers quickly, deftly, and his pants legs fell away. Another zip and he was open at the rear. "*Komm hierher,*" he whispered to the man, who moved forward soundlessly, mechanically, his glasses glittering. "*Aber erst einen Kuss,*" Eckermann said, tilting up his head.

The man leaned over and kissed him lightly, then reached into a can on the floor and began to grease his handless forearm. I looked back only once, but the crowd had closed in around the sling.

I didn't open the square of paper, folded into the pocket of my nylon jacket, until I got downstairs. The spiky lettering seemed very far away. It was slow work making sense of it. Even when understood, the words didn't form into thoughts with any suddenness or surprise. How could they?

The name on the paper was Hamilton Thorpe. There was no escape. Not for him, not for me.

X. Hamilton

Avery was still asleep, his long body curled into a fetal crouch, facing away from me. I reached over him to the table and fished for a cigarette. Let him sleep. I'd kept him up almost until dawn, after stumbling in from the Hellhole. He had looked at the slip of paper, listened to my ravings, and returned me to reality. Finally I slept. Not well. There were dreams — lurid spectaculars — that lit my skull and brought me awake a few hours later, still exhausted.

He muttered something about strawberries. I shoved my leg alongside his. He was like a little oven. I bent over, forgetting my concern for his sleep. I don't want to be alone, I thought, wake up. But he only muttered again, this time about peaches. His eyelids, translucent blue flaps, quivered.

I lay back, inhaling harmfully. The light filtering through the green shades turned the room into a subaqueous gloom. We might have been under water. What nonsense. My mind was jumping around. I needed to concentrate.

Sometime between sleeping and waking, I had discovered the next step. Maybe it had come in one of those nightmares. Maybe the tooth fairy had left it under my pillow. But it was there when I woke up, a nubbin of a plan.

Wake up, I thought again, I need you. I kicked him. He whimpered and went on sleeping.

I couldn't really think about it. It was too strange. Too fantastic. It had nothing to do with me. With Cord McGreevy, school teacher, dog-lover, friend. It belonged to someone else, whom I hadn't met yet. Or glimpsed once in a smoky mirror. What was it my mother said when she caught us doing things she disapproved of? "Nice people don't do things like that."

Nice people. Well, nice people didn't drip hot wax on their lovers or lie about homecoming dates. Or murder people. I was confusing things, perhaps, but still, the truth was there, underneath the rambling. The rules of the game weren't what they used to be. As my mother liked to think.

Avery was waking up. My brainwaves must have disturbed his sleep. I bent down and whispered into the shell of his ear. "Good morning." I felt dangerously manic.

He flopped over on his back and the native hue of resolution returned to his face. "Awrggh," he said.

"Know what you were doing? Cutting up fruit salad. Peaches. Strawberries. God knows."

"Uh-uh."

"Yes you were."

"Playing a slot machine. Oh God. Lemons won. What time is it?"

"Time to get up."

"I'm going back to sleep." He pulled the covers up to his eyes but I yanked them off and lowered my mouth to his belly-button. I blew into it hard, making farting noises.

"Cut that out!"

"Up!" I lowered my head again and emptied my lungs.

He groaned and twisted and fell on the floor.

When I came out of the bathroom he was in his black Japanese housecoat, yawning over the electric perc. My mind had been busy in the bathroom, cutting my plan into its component parts. I didn't know yet. It hadn't come together. But it was trying. When the coffee was poured, I started in, my head a swirl of energy.

"You're gonna think this is crazy. But it's the only way I can be sure. Absolutely sure. But I need your help. At first." I paused, watching him work up his objections, then jumped in again. "Don't think Hamilton isn't one step ahead of us. He's been ahead of us from the beginning. We're gonna put him on tape." Avery's baffled expression changed to curiosity. I had him "Yep. Tape. Tape everything he says, right in this apartment. Sound too. Gotta have the words. I want you to arrange it. With your trusty Brownie."

Avery shook his head slowly while I went into details. At the same time I knew I had him hooked.

"On tape and on audio. The only way a jury will know. Don't forget, he'll have a good lawyer. The best. And what've we got? A date. A name on a piece of paper. A piece of plastic."

Avery sighed, then let out a soundless whistle. "I didn't

figure on a one-reeler with the Keystone Kops right in my own living room."

"It's not the Keystone Kops at all. This is for real. Life and death." I felt marvelously light-headed. I was on a plane that had a life, a logic, all its own. Best of all, it didn't intersect with the ground.

"You know, Cord, it sounds a little... freaked out. I mean, why not give the cops a chance? Now that you've got this evidence...."

"I told you! They don't want to solve this case! They dropped it twenty-four hours after they started! They're not interested in this kind of crime. Maybe they want us to kill each other off!"

His eyes went dark at that. I guess he was debating the finer points of paranoia. I could hardly blame him.

"Well, when? When do you want to do it?"

"Today. This afternoon."

He stood up and went to the window. His back was broad enough to block most of the light. When he turned his voice was flat and uninflected. Avery the technician speaking.

"We won't be able to use the spots. That means lower light values. From the window, the lamps. Definition will be off."

"Doesn't matter, just so long as we can identify the speaker. And the voice."

He looked at the sofa where I was sitting. "The built-in mike isn't sensitive enough. We're talking about twenty-five feet. I'll have to jack in an extra, run it over."

I looked around. There was a Moorish lantern of perforated brass in one corner of the room. I picked it up and placed it in front of the couch, under the coffee table. "This here and the mike inside."

He nodded. "Okay."

"Now. What about turning the damn thing on? Also the noise?"

"I'll run a remote control into the bedroom. I can find some reason to go in and turn it on."

"I'll stay there. I can do it."

Our eyes met and I had the sensation he was only humoring me. Or stalling.

"The noise. H'mmm...." He chewed his lower lip.

"Put something loud on the stereo. They'd expect music anyway." He nodded. "You know, it might be better if you're not here. Not involved."

He shook his head. "You can't do it without me.'

"I only need you for the phone call."

"If you meet them at the door they won't even come in. They'll smell a rat."

"I can try."

He shook his head. "Negative. I'm with you, double-O. All the way."

He called the shop around noon and asked for Hamilton. I stood nearby, listening. His first request was made casually. The response seemed affirmative. The second request was made more hesitantly. He stumbled once or twice. His pause was longer this time, the goodbyes slightly strained. When he hung up his face was cloudy. "He said he'd see what he could do."

"Nothing specific?"

"No."

"He knew what you were getting at, right?"

Avery didn't answer, just kept his eyes pinned on me. I didn't want to know what he was thinking. At last he said, "You look kinda rocky, Cord, would you like a massage? Maybe it'll loosen you up."

I went over to window. Third Avenue, three floors down, was alive with shoppers. The most expensive flea market in the world. I tried to control the thudding of my heart. Could I be wrong? The only one wrong? No one was really convinced but me. Not Avery. Not Jared — probably not even if he knew about this last bit of information. I fought the urge to call him and tell him about Eckermann. What difference would it make? The decision was still mine. Mine alone.

And then, on cue, I recalled my last moment with Hamilton. Summoned up the sight of him standing in our group at the party, frozen into immobility while his eyes darted from one face to another. Gauging, measuring, confessing. Yes, confessing. There was a message in those pained eyes and I knew what it was. Even if I was the only one. I turned around.

"Come on," Avery said, stretching out a hand.

"I know I'm right. *I know it*."

"I'll turn your bones to rubber. My Dad taught me how."

He did for almost an hour. Then he laid his big warm hand on my forehead and breathed "Sleep" into my ear and, miraculously, I did.

The doorbell sounded at 4:15. Everything was ready. High pings from a synthesizer were barreling out of the stereo. The line for the extra mike ran under three scatter rugs. The mike itself, a bubble of sensitivity, was tucked inside the Moorish lantern. The switch to the whole assembly was in the bedroom.

Avery and I traded one last look after the buzzer stopped. I could see his nostrils dilate. Ever since I woke up from my nap I'd been asking myself what right I had to involve him in my amateur sleuthing. If something went wrong, if there was violence, he would suffer — without ever having laid eyes on Ellison. But the sound of his calm voice, the sure movements of his hands, stopped me. There was no use pretending. I couldn't have done it without him. I went in the bedroom, closing the door almost completely.

"It's wonderful of you to invite us." Hamilton's voice was warm and emphatic. Paul murmured something. Hamilton continued."We were both terribly tired. Saturday's our busy day. A madhouse. But we wanted to be with you."

"Well," Avery's voice was strained, "we had that date a few weeks ago."

"Oh yes," Paul sounded high and brittle. "The night Cord was over. " A pause. Then lightly, "You seen much of him?"

"A little, yeah. Not too much."

Hamilton intervening. "He's a sweetheart. A real favorite of ours. Isn't he, angel?"

"Yes he is."

I had the momentary impression that all this was dialogue from the track of an old movie. The same brittle falseness, hidden meanings.

"You have a beautiful place, Avery." This from Paul. The voices were nearer now. "I love wicker furniture sprayed white. Your accents work beautifully. Can we see the rest of the apartment?"

I tensed but Avery handled it well. "All my film junk is in there. Just a workroom really. I don't usually show it."

I heard the couch squeak. "We'd love a drink, Avery." From Hamilton. Then he raised his voice. "You know what today is? Our tenth anniversary. I met Paul ten years ago today." Avery murmured something. I heard him walk toward the kitchen. Then the clink of glassware. "Ten years and he's just as sexy as ever."

Paul laughed — a high nasal sound. Hamilton continued.

"I was in Sloane's, looking for a chair. And this gorgeous young man waited on me. I ended up buying half the furniture on the floor just so I wouldn't have to leave."

136

Paul laughed, a pleased sound. "Come on, Hamilton."

"Do you remember Paul's legs? Sexy dancer legs." I heard the couch creak rhythmically.

Avery was back in the living room. His voice was light and casual. "Here you go."

"And I said to myself, that's someone special. Very special. And when I found out he was from Idaho I knew I wanted to spend the rest of my life with him."

Avery's voice was polite. "Idaho?"

"Only the best people come from Idaho."

Paul laughed again. "Oh come on."

"Only trouble is, they can never get the paint remover out from their knuckles. Show him, angel."

Paul whinnied. "I've been working in the basement all day."

"Ten years and everything he touches turns to gold. And he's still sexy as hell. Stand up, angel, let Avery see your ass."

I heard Avery clearing his throat. Another pause. Then Paul, lightly, "Why don't we... um... get started? We really should be back at the shop in time for..."

"Never mind that, angel." Hamilton's voice was low, commanding. I kept my eyes on the floor in the bedroom. The cracks between the flooring strips were filled with reddish dust. "We've got lots of time. Don't worry about the time, Avery."

"Okay."

More movements. I kept my eyes on the floor.

"I forgot to ask you..." Avery's voice again, too casual.

"What?"

"Did you bring anything with you?"

"Sure did. Poppers. We love poppers. Even though you're not supposed to use them any more."

"That's cool."

"Does this couch open up?" From Paul.

"Ahhh... no. I was in the mood for... ah... something kinky this afternoon." A nervous laugh.

I could hear a sharp intake of breath. "Like what?"

"I don't know. Just... kinky. Tired of the same old thing, maybe."

The room was silent except for *Fascinatin' Rhythm* rising insanely from the stereo. I shifted my weight. The silence resumed. Finally Hamilton: "We don't go in for far-out things. Just plain old sex. C'mere."

"Really." More silence. I imagined them frozen into position, a courting ritual suddenly gone awry.

At last, from Hamilton, "We brought something just in case. But we don't usually..."

"What?"

From Paul: "We found out about it in Europe." He snickered slightly.

"What is it?"

"Show him, angel."

I stepped to the crack in the door. Paul dug into his pocket. Everything went into slow-motion — the hand withdrawing, the fingers unfolding, the plastic device glistening in the center of his palm. There was a long dangerous moment while the synthesizer went into *The Planets*. Avery was waiting for me. I pushed at the tiny panel in my hand. I heard very faint clicks. Then I swung the door wide.

They sensed me first, of course, perhaps following Avery's glance. Hamilton, on the couch, looked up. His face hardened. Paul closed his hand and held it high, as if trying to ward off a blow.

"What the hell!" Hamilton stood up. "What is this?" He looked from me to Avery and back. Avery was trembling. I found myself surprisingly calm.

"I wanted to find out something," I said, "and now I have."

"Come on, Paul."

"Just a minute. First I want to show you something."

"Don't want to see it. Come on."

I moved between them and the front door, holding out my hand. It was closed.

"You have no right, Cord." Hamilton was more deeply angry now, scarlet mounting to his forehead. "I don't know what's wrong with you but you have no right to come here. And act like this."

"I'm sorry. I have every right." I opened my hand and they looked. "Do you know where I found this?" A long wait as their eyes moved to my face. "In Ellison's bedroom. With proof that it was used the night he was murdered."

Hamilton's eyes narrowed into pinpoints. "Damn you," he said, "you go to hell."

Paul turned away, like an object arrested in flight. Suddenly Hamilton slumped and I knew the first round was mine.

"You lied about your arrival time, didn't you? Go on, admit it. You lied about a lot of things. Like saying you arrived too late to be of help. Like learning from Marta at the switch-board that he was dead."

Hamilton moved to Paul and put his arm around his shoulder. I'm sorry, angel," he murmured. Paul stood trans-fixed, his face marble-white. Hamilton turned toward me again. His voice was infinitely weary. "You're on the wrong track, Cord. You should be ashamed of yourself."

"If I'm on the wrong track, tell me how. You're the only one who can."

He looked at Paul again. "If you'll turn off that horrible racket, I will."

I nodded to Avery. He went to the stereo and turned the volume down slightly. Hamilton collapsed on the sofa. I could hear the camera whirring now, but they didn't seem to notice.

"I'm not a liar, Cord. You should know me well enough. After all these years. Yeah, the ship docked that Saturday. We got home before noon. To tell you the truth, we didn't even know you and Ellison were back. We hadn't heard from you, hadn't been in touch since we saw you off."

"Are you telling me you weren't with Ellison that night?" I could see the signs of a vicious inner struggle. He clenched and unclenched his hands, his chest rising and falling. He glanced at Paul. "I should tell you, I've got proof."

"Save your proof. I'll tell you. Are you listening?" His rage flew out. "You've got this whole fucking thing figured out! *Are you listening?*"

"I'm listening, Hamilton."

As he talked he calmed down, the anger smoothing away into sorrow.

"Yes I was. For a short time. An hour, no more. Ellison called me at home that night. I think he just took a chance that we were back. He didn't know for sure. Paul was asleep at the time." Hamilton raised his eyes to Paul, who was still standing, his spine curved almost like a bow. "He asked could I come over. He was very depressed. He said your summer in Italy had been a bomb."

I tensed. The unspoken accusation.

"I told him I couldn't. He begged me. Really begged. I . . . I couldn't say no." He closed his eyes, his lashes fluttering. "Ellison and I . . . I couldn't say no, that's all."

It was Paul who broke the gathering silence. "Tell them. It's okay, tell them."

I wanted to shout at the idea, smother it, but it swelled

until it occupied all the space in my head. Hamilton looked at me, his face stony. "You didn't think those tennis games were for real, did you?"

I looked at him, afraid to breathe for the noise it would make.

"It started in the fall. Just over a year ago. When you got back from Yugoslavia. I went to see him one night. Paul and I had had a spat. Just to talk. He was in rotten shape. All fucked up. He'd had dinner with you. You were just using him. Taking and taking and never giving."

A lie, I thought, *a stinking rotten lie.*

"We were drinking. Lots. It doesn't matter now, but that's how it started." He looked at me and shook his head. "Don't get me wrong. I'm not saying you got us started. That wouldn't be fair. We knew what we were doing."

Avery came over and sat on the floor next to my chair. His hand moved to mine. He began to rub very softly.

"We didn't see each other all that often. Paul and I... we'd made it up, of course. But still, Ellison was... you know what he was." He paused. "Like a big bowl of sugar. Brown sugar. I thought... stupid... I could include both of them. Give them both what they wanted. Stupid! You can't do that. Nobody can. Ellison knew I'd gone back to Paul even before I did. That's why he canceled out on Spoleto. He didn't want to hurt Paul any more. God!" He turned away sharply. "He was one beautiful person."

Everything seemed to have settled into slow motion, even the rubbing of Avery's hand on mine.

"That night. He was all upset when I got there. Caged. Crazy. Maybe he was on something, I don't know. He said he was getting out of gay life. Said it was for shit. Had a new gig, something like that. It didn't make much sense. I tried to cheer him up. But he knew what was happening with me. Me and Paul. He always knew. I was just leaving when... he came at me. Like a child. An orphan. It was..." his voice sank to a whisper, "...I couldn't say no. I broke my promise. The promise I made to my angel."

Paul broke his silence softly. "I knew you had. I knew where you were."

"I left around midnight. I don't know what the police told you. If they said he was killed before midnight they were lying. He came out to the banister as I walked downstairs. I'll never forget. Standing there. Just in a towel. He looked like a... a stonecutter's masterpiece. I'm sorry." He looked at Paul and shook his head. "He was a beautiful man."

The sun had dropped behind the buildings across the street, turning the room moth-colored.

"That thing. I'd brought it along as a gag. Just to amuse him. It was a duplicate we'd made from a rubber glove. This one," he pointed to Paul, still clutching the device, "was the original. It came from one of the sex shops in Europe. We used it once or twice there."

Avery lay against me, his eyes closed. I could see the pulse beating in his neck.

"When I left Ellison... that last time... I had the feeling something was going to happen to him. Something terrible. He couldn't keep on the way he was. He was burning out." He brushed his hand across his face. His eyes were red. "And that, so help me God, is the truth."

I don't know how long we sat there, numb with our private griefs, as the room got darker. And then, unexpectedly, the stereo switched off. The side had ended. The whirring of the camera was very audible.

Hamilton blinked once or twice, then got up and went to the source of the sound. Then he turned on his heel and came back, standing over me. I didn't cringe. Not even when he lifted his arm. It was Avery who stopped him.

"Oh my God, Cord, the police!" We looked at him. His eyes were huge. "This afternoon. While you were asleep. I told them about... about everything. I thought they should know. For insurance! Oh, I'm so sorry! I'm so sorry!"

"No," Hamilton's face seemed very far away, a pinpoint in the dusk, "I didn't kill Ellison. You were wrong. And now you've made a fucking mess of everything."

"If you didn't," I cried, "then for the love of God *who did?*"

The words decayed slowly in the violet room. Then we all turned in the direction of the entrance hall. Jared Green was there. He stepped forward. The scars on his face were glowing horribly, as if he were peppered with blood. He looked at each of us in disgust.

"You'll have to ask Liz Garrity," he said. "She was Ellison's wife, a long time ago, and I have a hunch she was with him the night he died."

XI. Jared

Avery turned on the lamps. Jared stepped into the room. No one spoke as Jared sat down and asked for a drink. Avery went into the kitchen. When he returned with a tumbler of gin, Jared took three sips before beginning.

"Your assistant at the shop told me you were here. He said it was a social call." Jared's eyes hooded down briefly, tactfully. "He also said Avery and Cord had met one night at your place. That was all I needed to know. I figured he'd be mixed up in all this."

Jared swiveled his glance to me. I couldn't meet it.

"After he waltzed out of your party last night I figured something like this would happen. I know the way his mind works."

"Too bad you didn't clue us in," Hamilton's voice was heavy with irony. Jared sighed and sipped his tumbler of gin.

I cleared my throat. "Liz Garrity. Would you mind. . .?"

"I'm coming to that." He polished off the gin and set down the glass. Then he reached in his pocket and produced a photograph. "I bought the bureau in the bedroom, remember? The oak dresser with the mirror. I didn't need it but I bought it anyway. I don't even remember what I paid."

"Fifty dollars," I said dully. I remembered writing the ticket.

"Fifty dollars. Well. It's been sitting in my front vestibule ever since. This morning I took a good look at it. Opened the drawers, threw away the old liner paper." He waved the photo. "This was underneath, top middle drawer. It must have been there for years."

He handed me the snap. I recognized Ellison at once.

Younger, slimmer. Strangely eager, a quick grin on his face, a grin that seemed to plead *Like me, like me*... He had grinned like that the night I first met him.

The girl lying next to him on the beach towel was familiar but I had to look hard to see the resemblance. She was slimmer then too, her features oddly sharp. But mostly it was the hair that put me off. A glossy chestnut instead of blond.

"I didn't connect until about an hour ago," Jared continued. "It hit me while I was mopping the kitchen floor. I'd been reaching for it but every time it got away. All of a sudden, there it was."

I turned the photo over. On the back, in Ellison's downhill writing, *Princess Hotel, Bermuda*. And a date. Ten years ago, almost to the day.

"Then I started figuring it out," Jared said. "The dates. Ellison came to the bank eight years ago. He was just out of school. Said he'd gotten a divorce a few months before and that he'd been married two years. That tallies exactly with the date on the photo. They went to Bermuda on their honeymoon."

"My God," Hamilton breathed.

"So we have to ask ourselves, why did he keep his former relationship with this woman a secret? Why didn't he tell us his wife had re-entered his life?" Jared looked around, stopping at me. I stared at him stupidly. "Something must have prevented him. What could it have been?"

"Maybe," this from Paul, "they decided to get back together."

"Well obviously something was going on between them. Something they didn't want publicized."

"No way," I said at last. "Ellison would've told me."

"Good God, Cord, his ex-wife was teaching in the same school — he probably got her the job — and he didn't tell you. Use your head!"

I looked around the circle of faces. They were watching me. Agreement was plain on all their faces. I was off and running with one of my half-baked theories.

"Why don't you let somebody else put two and two together, Cord," Hamilton's voice was harsh. "You've had your turn."

"Yeah, you did." An echo from Paul. I turned away.

"Okay, Liz and Ellison were married once and they wanted it to be a secret. Why? Next question — why didn't Liz turn up at the funeral in New Jersey? Rivkin knew about it and he said he had contacted the teachers who were in the city. And we know she was here. She'd arrived by ship the weekend before." He paused ironically. "The famous crossing of the QE2. Okay, third. Why didn't she come to the furniture sale? It was advertised — notice in the faculty room, telephone networking, everything. Several people asked for her, I remember. But she stayed away. Odd, don't you think?"

No one replied and Jared went on. "We have to get the answers. From her."

"What are you saying, Jared?" I glared at him. "That Liz had something to do with Ellison's murder?"

"Not necessarily." He spread his hands. Under his confident manner I read confusion. "But I'd like the answers to those questions."

"Wait a minute!" Hamilton hunched forward. "I just remembered. There was a phone call while I was there!"

"While you were where?" Jared's voice was sharp, almost shrill. He listened as Hamilton filled him in, interrupting only once to ask for a refill of gin. When Hamilton finished, he asked, "What was the phone call?"

"Ellison was in the can. I didn't know whether to pick up or not. About the sixth ring I did. It was a woman. She said... she didn't say, she just screamed. 'Who is this?' And before I could say anything she hung up."

We sat silently, digesting that information.

"It could've been... anyone." My words hung foolishly in the air.

Jared looked at me. "One of his many lady friends."

"He had lady friends, yeah. There was Mary Battaglia, Minnie Graef..."

"And these were the kind of people who would call him around midnight?"

I subsided, thinking about Liz. I knew her, they didn't.

"By the way," Jared turned to Avery, "I heard you say the police were... informed. What are they going to do?"

Avery looked anguished. "They're coming over."

Hamilton jerked at this but said nothing.

"What time?" Jared continued.

"About six."

"I see. You figured you'd have all the evidence by then." Jared nodded. "Sherlock Holmes and Watson." He checked his watch. "It's five-thirty now." He looked at Hamilton. "Maybe you should leave."

"No." Hamilton's voice was firm. "I want it out right

here." He looked at Avery. "Did you tell the cops about your spy machines?" Avery closed his eyes. "I see. That takes care of that."

"We can destroy the tape right now," I said.

"Don't bother. I'm going to tell the same story. At least they'll know I told it voluntarily the first time."

"Anyway," Jared said, "I think Cord and I should leave before they get here. To have it out with Liz. The sooner the better as far as you and the police are concerned."

"I couldn't agree more," Hamilton said dryly.

"Okay, Cord, let's go." Jared stood up. His second tumbler of gin was empty. He seemed to expand slightly. I kissed Avery before heading for the door. Turning, I saw that Paul had moved next to Hamilton and was holding his hand, his falcon face pointed at him.

"By the way," Jared said, opening the apartment door, "I strongly recommend you keep this door locked when you're in residence. Next time it might not be a friend who drops in."

Our departure was just in time. We saw Drosky and Buzzini looking for a parking space in front of Avery's building. They were in an unmarked car. I ached at the thought of the questions Hamilton would have to answer.

Liz lived in one of those hybrid blocks near Lincoln Center, handy to the opera houses, a block that was a blend of brownstones and soaring glass towers. We hardly spoke in the taxi. Jared held himself tensely, trying to second-guess the driver's whipsaws through traffic. I was tense too — but with remorse, confusion. I didn't want to risk Jared's irony by speaking.

Her house was of granite, with gargoyles grinning evilly from the lintels. Her name under the bell was lettered in a florid, cursive script. She lived on the parlor floor. There was a long wait after we rang, an even longer wait after I announced myself on the intercom.

She met us at the door of the apartment. "Cordell!" She gave out a squeal of pleasure and turned to Jared. "And Jared! From last night! See, I remembered and I'm terrible at names!"

I knew her apartment would be vaguely theatrical, but I wasn't prepared for this. The windows had been covered with translucent gels, cut into intricate designs and taped together to resemble stained glass. The light that filtered through was smoky with blues and yellows and reds. The walls were hung with heavy drapes, plum-colored velvet with heraldic signs sewn on with gold thread. There were stagey objects lying around — halberds, a gold crown, military boots, a curving sword. The whole place looked like the prop department of an opera workshop.

She led us to a drawing board. Push-pins held a dozen sketches in place. "You caught me working on my new opera. Anne of Austria. Most interesting woman in Europe. More interesting than Elizabeth or Christina or Mary of Scotland... everybody."

"Anne of Austria?" I looked at the costume sketches. The runny style was unpleasantly familiar. "I never heard of her."

"Oh Cordell, where have you been?"

As she gushed on, giving dates, countries, genealogies, I watched her, trying to match the swollen face before me with the girlish one of the photo. The bluish-gray eyes were the same but almost everything else had changed. And then, looking at her, I had the sudden impression, so vague as to be hardly graspable, that she reminded me of someone else altogether. Who?

"I don't know *why* nobody thought of doing an opera about Anne of Austria before. Well, I'm doing the libretto and the costumes and the sets. Everything except the music." She trilled a few bars, quite prettily, then named a well-known composer. "He's seen two of my poems and composed the arias already. We're trying to get foundation money." She turned to Jared, who had said very little. He was looking at a framed sketch on the wall. "You can't do anything without a grant, isn't that right, Jared? You're a businessman, you ought to know. Oh that. That was for my production at the Staatsoper in Munich. The second act of *Fledermaus*. The party. Like it?"

"Very nice. I didn't realize you were such a successful stage designer. Cord didn't tell me."

A windy sigh. "Cordell never tells anybody anything. He likes to keep everything secret."

"Yes," Jared agreed, coming back, "he does that."

"What can I get you folks to drink? Or eat?"

Jared removed a music box from a chair and sat down. The box began to tinkle out the opening bars of *Eine Kleine Nachtmusik*. "A drink, if you've got it," he said.

"I'm going to give you each a glass of scuppernong wine."

He closed his eyes in what appeared to be pain and nodded. While she was in the kitchen he kept his eyes on the floor. I roamed round, looking at the props.

She came back with a decanter and three glasses, heavy

leaded crystal with gold rims. "You'll love this, " she said, "it's from Mother's Vineyard."

"Your mother makes scuppernong wine?" I asked, on cue.

She giggled. "No, that's the name of the brand." She poured the wine, then went back to the drawing board. "I just sent a whole bunch of sketches to Alfredo Portacci." She looked at us triumphantly. She seemed to have expanded in the last few minutes. Or perhaps it was her costume — a long blue robe, dotted with silver stars, its sleeves like cornucopias. She had worn that dress to school once, for a faculty meeting, but now it seemed more outrageous and, in this light, more eerie. She might have been a sorcerer's apprentice. "You know who Alfredo Portacci is?" We looked at her. "He's production manager at La Scala! That's where they did my *Francesca da Rimini* year before last! Didn't I tell you about that?"

I shook my head very slowly, trying to keep the realization, from taking shape in my head. I'd been wrong about everything so far. I couldn't trust my judgment now, not about this...

Jared swirled the wine around in his glass. When he spoke his voice was mild. "You remember what we were talking about at the party last night? About Cord being suspicious of Hamilton and Paul?"

"Yes I do. And aren't you sorry?" She turned toward me.

"Well," Jared continued, "he was right. They did lie about their arrival. They're with the police now."

Her eyes grew round. "Hamilton and Paul?" She moved away from the drawing board. "I can't believe it."

"I can't either. But it looks like Cord was right."

"Well do tell." She sat down, arranged her gown in folds, and sipped her wine.

"Hamilton admitted he visited Ellison the night he died."

She looked up swiftly at that. Jared went on.

"They may ask you to confirm that."

The silence was immense. Her voice, when it came out, was high and girlish. "Me?"

"Yes. Hamilton said you called Ellison that night and hung up as soon as you heard his voice."

I held on, refusing to judge.

"I don't believe I ever called Ellison in my life."

"You sure?"

"I'm so bad at names, I've even forgotten what his last name was. I couldn't have looked it up in the book."

There was a moment while we waited. My flesh prickled. "Have some more scuppernong wine," she said at last.

Jared didn't reply. I felt, rather than saw, the photograph being taken out. For one instant I wished myself miles away, in a place where people could never be caught in lies, where the truth would never shame anyone.

"That's strange," his words sailed across the room, "since it was your own name once."

She looked from one of us to the other, then her tiny hands balled into fists. "*My* name?"

He handed her the snapshot. She took it, her face blank, and bent her head. When she looked up, her lower lip was slanted across her jaw. She handed the photograph back. We waited. At last Jared said, more gently, "Is that you?"

She stood up, full-breasted in the center of the room. No longer the sorcerer's apprentice but the wizard herself. Then she started walking around, touching her properties as if they were magic talismans. "You know nothing about it... absolutely nothing!" Her voice was low and rushed. "You come here and you think you can say anything and get me all upset. When you don't really know anything. Nothing! You hear?" She wheeled at us, her face bulgy with anger. "What do you know about Ellison? Really?"

"We were his friends for a long time," Jared murmured.

"I was his friend before he knew any of you! Before... before..." her face was suddenly murderous, "he knew any of you daffodils!"

The words slammed around the room. *Oh no*, voices shouted in my ear, *not that, not that kind of hatred from Liz...*

"Daffodils?" Jared sounded amused. "Do you mean homosexuals?"

"You know what I mean, I don't have to tell you. Ellison was a man! A man!"

"The two terms aren't mutually exclusive."

"Don't gimme any of that New York double-talk, you know what I mean." She went to a gold crown and picked it up. It glittered in the subdued light. "Don't think I don't know about you, Cordell McGreevy." She wheeled toward me. "Living down there in the Village. I knew about you right off, right from the beginning. I saw you walking down the hall and I knew. Ellison didn't even have to tell me."

I wrenched away from the ugliness of the words but she went on. "Why do you think he got in touch with me? Got me to come to New York? Because he wasn't what you all made him out to be. You were the one he hated most of all," she hissed. "Cord McGreevy, Class A faggot."

Jared gestured to me and I was still.

"You know when he told me he hated you?" She spread her arms, the heavy blue sleeves hanging down like flags. "When he came to visit me in Rome. While you were on Capri. Came and stayed with me and we never left the hotel room. You know what we were doing, Cordell McGreevy? You know?" She threw back her head. "Don't make me laugh. *You'll never know.*"

Jared signaled me again but the time to be silent was past. "You were going to help Ellison get rid of his faggot friends, is that it?"

"Sure I was. That's what he wanted." She stopped and drew herself up proudly. "I don't know why I'm telling you this. We agreed not to. Not to let you in on what we were doing. It was none of your business."

"Are you sure Ellison wanted that? Wanted me not to know?"

She bared her teeth triumphantly. "Did he tell you? *Did he!*"

She was right, of course. But there was something she didn't know. My complicity in that decision. I had helped create the Ellison who had turned away — the knowledge uncoiled in the dark where it had waited for so long. I had created him and now, in all fairness, I would have to dismantle him, shred away his poses and posturings and give him his revenge. On me. On her. On the world.

"Do you know why?" I was amazed at the mildness of my tone. I stared at her. She shied back, seeing some kind of sureness she couldn't handle.

"Now that you've got me all riled up..." she turned away, searching the draperies. "I think it's time you left. Both of you."

"I'm sorry we upset you," I went on agreeably, "but there's something you have to hear. Something about Ellison."

She started to hum under her breath but I went on talking. "You know what it is. You knew it when you married him. You knew it when you divorced him. And you knew it when you called his apartment that Saturday night and a man answered."

She broke away, moving to the back of the apartment, but my words followed her. "Ellison was a beautiful man and maybe he never found what he wanted, but if he had, it would have been with a man. We failed him, everyone failed him. But you failed him most of all because you helped him pretend."

She held the crown in front of her, her eyes blank and unseeing.

"Pretend, Liz, but pretending is what you're best at. I'm sorry, it's true. You never had an opera production in your life. Any more than you had the Ellison you thought you did. It was all an empty promise."

"You dirty liar," the words snaked out of the gloom. "I ought to kill you."

I laughed briefly. "Me too, Liz?"

Her face was a stain of white. She dropped the crown. It rolled into a corner. Then the answer came, heavy and toneless. "He didn't want me to save him. He was just like you. All of you. A rotten daffodil. I got rid of... scum!"

The words burned in the air for a moment and then the door behind her opened, revealing the bedroom in a ray of light. Minnie Graef looked at us.

"I want you to come in here, Elizabeth," she said, "your father will be back in a minute." Her hand went to her throat and I saw the delta of swollen blue veins. She looked at me. "I'm sorry, Cord, I'm so terribly sorry."

I don't know how long we stood there, trapped in silence, and then I saw Liz's heavy body falling and Minnie stooping down to cradle her and then two pairs of wounded blue-grey eyes looking up at us.

Of course. Minnie and Liz. Mother and child.

XII. Avery and Cord

Say it loud, gay and proud--- say it louder, gay and prouder!
The endlessly moving chain of women and men circled on 43rd Street, looped out to Times Square, then back again. Past knots of onlookers — some curious, some idle, some jeering.

"Okay brothers and sisters." A reedy-looking marshal wearing an armband with a pink lambda addressed us through a megaphone. "Let's do it again." He started the chant and we picked it up, faintly at first, then in a rising crescendo that must have reached the top of the skyscrapers on either side.

Hands pumped up and down the line in the power salute. I moved my arm in unison, submerged in the crowd's excitement. It had been a long time since I'd taken part in a demonstration. Bits of tickertape floated down from the windows above. We had friends in high places.

New York's finest stood around us, north and south, east and west. Some had riot gear — billies, shields, masks. I tried to read their faces, tried to find some sign of remorse. Police brutality had triggered this demonstration. They'd smashed a gay bar to pieces in this neighborhood. They'd smashed some of its patrons too. Just like the old days.

I looked at one cop carefully. He was young, with skin like new milk and hard blue eyes. He blinked as I stared, then his eyes glazed over. I saw his hand tighten on his white club, the knuckles straining. He tapped it against his thigh, a reflex. It occurred to me that the cops' job was not to protect us but to neutralize us, to shield the onlookers from our demands, from the justice of our claims.

I started to explain this to Avery but he had his eye on a van which had pulled into 43rd Street. I could see the CBS logo emblazoned on the side, the video camera on the roof. A technician was setting up; in a few minutes the red eye would light — a remote for the Six O'Clock News. A slight tremor of fear hit me. We'd have to walk past that red eye more than once. Every time around, in fact.

"Looks like nothing's gonna happen. Too bad, I got mine all picked out."

The words floated down from overhead. I looked up. A beefy mounted patrolman on a chestnut mare was surveying the scene. His buddy smiled. "Yeah. Me too."

A spasm of rage went through me. "Which one?" I shouted up, aware of faces turning around, of violence lurking.

The horse snorted and curvetted. The beefy cop's face was suddenly murderous. "It'll take more education than you got to know what's goin' through my mind!"

I glared at him, heart pounding. "Fuck you," I said.

Horse and rider started toward me, then were suddenly checked. They must have been under orders. Or was it the television camera, now swiveling toward us? Maybe they didn't want their mayhem recorded.

"Hey!" It was a sallow man in his mid-thirties, now keeping pace with me. "This is a non-violent demonstration."

"I know," I muttered, hurrying to close the gap in the line. "I just hate those bastards." I thought briefly of Drosky and Buzzini. Were the gays and cops to be adversaries forever? Condemned to circle each other through eternity, one watching and waiting, the other jeering and defying? Forever locked out of understanding, forever prejudiced?

Prejudice, oppression, intolerance. Knee-jerk words which obscured more than they revealed. Would there ever be an end? I thought of Ellison, Liz. There were so many forms for hatred. Then I tried to shake off the thought. Today was the day I would not remember. When I would keep my mind clear. Full of nothing. But, as Dr. Ash was fond of pointing out, it is not possible to think of nothing. Nothing began to encapsulate Liz and Ellison again. Ellison and Liz. And Cord. I was the third leg of the triangle.

The last few weeks had been busy and exhilarating. I'd spent more and more time at Avery's, settling into his apartment, wondering how I'd lived alone for so long. The best part of it was going to sleep at night. Holding Avery's wide bony hand in that big bed, setting forth together on the most dangerous journey of all, the journey to the bottom of night.

Knowing I didn't have to face my dreams alone.

Sometimes, as I embarked on that dark trip, that *mano a mano* through the arenas of sleep, I wondered if what Avery and I shared was "love." I had long ago learned to mistrust the word. It was too common a noun, too loaded with lies, and I stepped around it the way you would a trite remark or a bad joke. It seemed to have nothing to do with our life together — the grumpiness, the sudden elation, the jokes and cooking and fatigue, even the amazing sessions in bed, when I realized how right the ancient Egyptians were in declaring that human bones are made of silver and human flesh of gold. To give all that a name was to take away our specialness and join us to the lockstep of the world, to make us the last of a long line rather than the first. And so I avoided definitions. Even when Jared, visiting us one night for dinner, remarked in his savage way, "I feel good seeing you two so much in love," I felt a jolt of distaste. I didn't want to be classified that way, not by him, not by anyone. I think Avery felt the same way because he never referred to the subject — or the possibility — of love.

There had been the sessions with the Homicide people too. Drosky and Buzzini had been replaced by a higher-up named Burns, a small Scotsman with gray sideburns who smelled of lilac water. Not that I had much to contribute to the case. I think they were amused, or fascinated, by the plastic sleeve. It was new in the annals of kink — even for these masters. I spared them the more lurid details of my search.

During my last sessions with Burns I asked him what would happen to Liz. "That's up to the D.A. and the grand jury," he replied. "There are some extenuating circumstances and no witnesses."

"Even if she killed him," I said, "she was innocent." I explained — haltingly — the notion I had been nursing for the last few weeks. That Ellison had taunted her into the final act. Teased and mocked her until she took out the weapon in her purse — a stage dagger set with chunks of colored glass, a letter opener from the second act of *Tosca* — and aimed it directly at his heart. And in that final minute, as the darkness flung its scarf across his eyes, he had snapped his fingers one last time and died — or won.

When I finished, Burns shrugged and looked superior. "You tellin' me she's not a murderer?"

"No she's not, really."

He laughed curtly. "You mean before she killed her boyfriend she wasn't. Afterwards, sonny, she was. The act made her a murderer — get it? Pretty fuckin' simple, if you ask me."

I realized we had different definitions of guilt and innocence and let the matter drop.

I had talked to Minnie and Anson only once since that afternoon at Liz's in the hallway at the Criminal Courts Building on Centre Street. I was late getting there and the psychiatric testimony had just ended. It had not yet been decided if Liz was legally competent to stand trial. Minnie gave me a fierce hug, her thin body clamped to mine. Paul stood by, looking sheepish and hangdog. I wanted to apologize to him but I didn't really know how, so I merely pressed his hand tightly. Perhaps he got my meaning, because he patted me twice, lightly, on the shoulder.

We stood without speaking for quite a while, each of us not wishing to intrude on the other's grief, until at last Minnie said, "There are things you have a right to know, Cord." She began to speak in a monotone. The attorney and reporters and guards hurrying past us were no doubt used to such intense huddles.

Elizabeth was the child of her first marriage. Lloyd Garrity had been a charmer, a deserter. After six years together he'd gone up to Maine from their home in Worcester and notified her he wasn't coming back. Getting child-support out of him had been a running battle. Eventually he had disappeared and she'd raised her daughter alone, giving up her own hope of becoming an artist, working instead in real estate, behind counters, in bookshops. When Elizabeth was fifteen, a rebellious girl with one pregnancy behind her, Minnie had met Anson. He lived alone, a divorced man. After they married they started an art supply business in Worcester, made it a success.

When Elizabeth brought Ellison to Worcester — by that time she was in college — they had liked him at once. "You couldn't help liking him," Minnie said, her blue-gray eyes lighting up, "he was dying to be liked." The phrase was unwelcome and she hurried on. "We had misgivings, of course, but he seemed good for Elizabeth. Calmed her down, understood her. Maybe he got her mind off her own difficulties. She had this wild ambition to design opera sets, and no patience with the delays involved. Still, they seemed happy. . . ."

"The gay thing changed all that," Anson cut in. "She

couldn't handle it. After they separated she had an. . . episode. She had to be hospitalized in California." His eyes searched mine, as if I had some answer. "It was partly hereditary, the doctors said. A predisposition."

Minnie spoke softly. "Lloyd had an aunt who'd had some trouble."

The hospitalization had been brief, and Liz had gone back to teaching, still in California. But when she notified her parents that she was coming back east, to New York, they decided to sell their shop in Worcester. They'd wanted to try their luck in the New York art world for many years. Now, with their daughter coming back, the time seemed right. It was only when they were all here that Liz told them she was seeing Ellison again — had gotten a job in his school, in fact.

"That's where you came in, Cord." Minnie's eyes were huge and troubled. "You were. . . I guess you know better than us."

"I was the competition," I said softly, "only I wasn't."

"It was all quite confused. I think Ellison played you off against her." She shook her head. "He was not a simple man."

"No, he wasn't."

"We told him about her being hospitalized in California. That he and Elizabeth weren't good for each other. We told her too, more than once." Minnie took out her hankie and blew her nose. The lines in her face were deeply etched. "I don't know, maybe it was all unavoidable, as if they were bound to destroy each other right from the beginning."

I turned away, embarrassed by the confusion showing on my face. Yes, I was part of it. The third leg of the triangle. Did Minnie and Anson know that? Or know it only partly? Was it my duty to fill them in on the details?

They had been glad Liz wanted to go to Europe this past summer. Thought it would get her away from Ellison, widen her horizons. They never dreamed she and Ellison would have a rendezvous.

"We didn't know at first." Anson shook his head. "Until she turned up with a shirt. And Ellison, when he came by. . ."

". . .the last time we saw him. . . ."

". . .let slip that he'd given her that shirt in Venice."

I breathed deeply. "Not Venice. Rome."

They looked at me curiously but I said no more. What was there to say?

Once their suspicions had been aroused they had kept

after Liz. There had been nasty scenes. Her old patterns had begun to appear. A doctor had been called in. But it wasn't until that last afternoon, when Jared and I had turned up, that she had told them the full story.

She'd been working late on sketches for a new opera. She'd been very excited about it, couldn't sleep. She had called Ellison — they often talked by phone late at night — to discuss a problem with staging. But this time someone else answered his phone. A man. He wouldn't identify himself.

One of her bad spells had started. She'd thrown on some clothes and gone downtown. But Ellison, when she got there, was adamant. Claimed he'd been alone. Told her she was invading his privacy, trying to take over his life. It was a re-play of their old trouble, the trauma that had led to her first breakdown. She lost control, claiming he'd betrayed her. There had been a screaming match, accusations, recrimina-tions...

Minnie and Anson stopped speaking. The same image danced in all our heads. Suddenly I recalled my theory that Ellison had mocked her, taunted her, into the final act. That it was as much suicide as murder. Would it make them feel better to hear it?

Just then their attorney walked up to us, a middle-aged man in a toupee. Our conversation would have to end. Still, there was one last question I wanted to ask. "Why didn't Elli-son tell me who you were? He took me around to meet you last spring but he didn't say a word."

Minnie spread her hands. Her eyes were red-rimmed. "Ellison," she echoed. "Who knows? He was a very strange, a very complicated man."

The chanting on the street had grown in volume while I was wool-gathering. Our numbers had grown to almost a thousand now. Another van had joined the first, another major network had decided we were newsworthy. Both camera systems were trained on us now. I could feel my palms start to sweat. The first image — a dreary one — was of Mr. Rivkin sitting in front of the Six O'Clock News tonight. And then Rivkin fogged over, to be replaced by several of my students. And to my surprise, I saw them smiling. The Little People didn't draw lines around people. They went for other things. Real things. The Little People knew all the important items before they came to school. We taught them the things that didn't matter.

The most difficult part had been going to see Mrs. Greer, a responsibility that was mine alone. She had known Liz, of course, but what she thought of her was locked up or buried now, and I didn't dare disturb her memories. Nevertheless, I had to tell her — or try to.

The shades were all pulled down, giving the old frame house a blind look. Mrs. Greer was upstairs, her bedroom airless and dark. I wasn't sure she knew who I was until she repeated my name. "Cord-ell?" Her voice was high and singsong. "How is your mother?"

She had never met my mother but always asked about her, looking for that fragment of me that pertained to both. "Fine," I replied, "still out west." After that she lapsed into silence. I pulled my chair to the bed and took her hand. Her fingers were gold, like Ellison's, but duller, as if the burnish had worn away. I could hear her niece downstairs in the kitchen, fixing tea. We would have only a few moments alone.

"I met. . . I met Ellison's wife," I began. "Liz. Elizabeth." Her eyes were fixed on the ceiling. "Actually she teaches at the same school I do." The eyelids fluttered slightly. "Did you know that she and Ellison became. . . friendly again last year?"

No response. I went on.

"Yes. Um, whatever they quarreled about, they patched it up." Her fingers twitched in mine and I thought she might reply. I waited. "She's in some trouble now. The police. . . ." The fingers tightened a little. ". . . the police think she might have had something to do with. . ." I took a deep breath. ". . . something to do with Ellison's death."

She pulled at me until she had raised herself to a sitting position. Her face was sunken, a gilded mask from some ancient treasury.

"Death?" she cried. "Ellison dead? My son dead?" I moved to support her, cradling her shoulders with my arm. "My son ain't dead!" The words came out with surprising force. "He's gone home like a shootin' star!" She fell against me and I lowered her to the pillow. "Like a shootin' star," she whispered, spittle forming at the corners of her mouth.

Ellen came in just then and insisted on my letting her rest. I kissed Mrs. Greer goodbye and tiptoed out. I couldn't deny the swelling of relief that poured through me. I had tried. And failed, thank God.

"Two, four, six, eight--- gay is just as good as straight!"

157

An old chant had been taken out of mothballs, spruced up for the occasion.

Yes, I was the third leg of the triangle. Ellison's failure was my failure, Liz's last illness and anguish built on everything that had kept me from Ellison. But was I truly to blame? I had loved Ellison, loved him as my brother. Did I have to lay this last guilt on myself?

The answer swept through me, over the tramp of feet, accompanied — amazingly — by the sight of Dr. Ash wreathed in his pipesmoke, enshrined in his plastic Barcalounger. I had been afraid of love that came wrapped in the flesh! Not afraid of the body, not afraid of the spirit. . . afraid of both together! I had squandered my flesh in every corner of the city, at the same time I had gifted Ellison with my tenderest friendship. And, except for that first evening, they had not joined, had not merged. A phrase I had heard once — I couldn't remember where — rolled back over me. *Your colored mammy.* God! It was one of those nasty half-truths, with just enough justice in it to sting. Mammy. . . the fake mother. Ellison. . . the fake lover. True and untrue. But how it hurt! And now I could see — how clearly! — that in denying Ellison, my brother, my twin, I had denied myself.

I tried to remind myself that the failure was not entirely my own. I was the product of a certain time and place. The years in Troy had left things buried in me, seven cities of my self, each with its own fear and pain. There was only limited freedom from that, no matter how hard I struggled.

We were abreast of the milk-skinned cop again. He was still tapping his club against his thigh. His eyes were a pitiless blue. He seemed to know everything there was to know about the angry mob around him.

Limited freedom! A wave of anger swept through me. Why should I settle for any restraints, other than the ones I laid freely on myself?

The reedy marshal was talking to the crowd again.

"You lucky people." His words curled precisely through the megaphone. "How would you like some Whitman?"

"Cool it, Arthur," someone said.

But Arthur smiled and fished a book from his jacket pocket. The chants faded away as he began to speak. "Give me now libidinous joys only," he began, then stopped. "You're not listening," he screeched into the megaphone. Some whistles sounded then everyone quieted down. He started again. I found myself suddenly drugged by the words.

Give me now libidinous joys only,
Give me the drench of my passions, give me life
    coarse and rank,
Today I go consort with Nature's darlings,
    tonight too,
I am for those who believe in loose delights,
    I share the midnight orgies of young men,
I dance with the dancers and drink with the
    drinkers...

As the words skipped over our heads, like so many silver dollars, I looked at Avery beside me. His head was cocked to one side, his high clear face intent, his lids half-shuttering his eyes. Suddenly, for no reason, he seemed like a stranger. Someone I knew only barely. A world encountered but only partly explored. It occurred to me, for the first time, that one day I would cease to know him, even as slightly as I did now. He would be replaced by someone else. And suddenly I had a vision of many Averys, some with his face, some with other faces, standing on a rainbow bridge as far ahead as I could see. I would give to each of them all that I could — nothing held back. And they would all take their life from me, from my love and my body, and they would always be part of me, even after we had separated, my brothers, caught in an unending spirit-music of skin and bone and hand and thigh. And if that did not end my aloneness, it would be because nothing could, because that was part of me, the essential material from which I sprang. A sudden spurt of joy lodged in my throat. I would not be ashamed of my solitude either.

Arthur finished reciting and lowered the megaphone. "More!" someone shouted.

"That's all there is," he shouted back. He held up the volume of poems.

And then I knew what I had to do. Knew with terrifying clarity, even though I was afraid I couldn't. It was so difficult, so terribly difficult. But on our next pass, under the unblinking cameras, I would. No shirking. No shirking now, ever.

And when we came around and I saw the cameras trained on us, red eyes flashing, I reached for Avery's hand. He was surprised and resisted for an instant, then relaxed. I lifted our joined salute to the world. A double measure of loving friendship.

We had come a long way. From our secret cinema in his living room, which I had wanted to destroy, to co-starring parts in a movie to the world.

Our gesture took only a moment and I suppose no one noticed or cared very much. But it was enough for me. To know. To know that I had done it for Ellison. For Liz. For myself.

For every brave, aching son and daughter moving with us under the dark November sky.

THE END

AN AFTERWORD

I am often asked how I came to write *The Butterscotch Prince*. My answer usually amuses people. I sat down in January 1973 to write a gay porno novel for Greenleaf Classics Inc. of San Diego, a publisher I knew nothing about except that they had brought out a few gay thrillers and some high-class porno by Phil Andros. Since I was unemployed at the time, having just returned from a two-year teaching stint in Puerto Rico, I decided to give it a try. I figured it wouldn't be hard to do, since the formula was set and I had a fair experience of sleaze. In other words, I went slumming.

Six weeks later I mailed off the completed manuscript to Greenleaf (whose editorial staff, I was later told, consisted of several literary lesbians). In due course, the rejected book came back, together with a reply. This informed me that though my work evidenced a certain talent, I had not produced a pornographic novel, as required. Such novels, I was advised, opened with a sex scene of no less than five pages, and went on to detail a major erotic encounter in every subsequent chapter.

Looking over my manuscript, I realized a great many chapters didn't mention sex at all, let alone linger over it in loving and apocalyptic detail. I had bombed in the porno market. My spirits sank.

Fortunately, a friend and ex-lover, visiting from California, saw my gloom. He believed in the novel and offered to phone three literary agents, selected at random from the Yellow Pages. My only stipulation was that he mention its gay content — I didn't want to send it out under false pretenses. This he did and all three agents offered to look at the manuscript — a small miracle in itself, I now realize. The first agent to read it (he actually specialized in scholarly books, it turned out) passed it on to another, who then passed it to a third. The third agent, Warren Bayless, liked the book, interviewed me, and assured me he would find a major publisher for it. I remembered walking along Lexington Avenue in a daze afterward — was it possible that my novel, my gay porno novel, was going to make it into the legit world?

Well — sort of. It took Warren a full year to place the book and then it was not with a major hardcover house but with Pyramid Books, a publisher of original paperbacks (later absorbed into Harcourt Brace Jovanovich). But what amazed me was the careful consideration and thoughtful analysis the book received from editors at G.P. Putnam's, William Morrow and other traditional houses. Each decided in turn that the book was a little too hot to handle — the fact that the plot turned on a sexual device alarmed them, I was told. Still, I was encouraged and began to think about my novel anew. In time I saw that I had tended to disparage it because of its humble origins. It might have started as pornography but, in spite of my best efforts, the book had moved on to other, larger matters — self-acceptance, the problems of male-male intimacy, race, coming-out.

Unfortunately, the editor at Pyramid who had bought the novel left the company soon thereafter. The novel was assigned to another editor, who hadn't yet read it. This editor, Jeanne Glass, eventually wrote me that she considered the book "very powerful and very good." I looked forward to a pleasant working relationship with her.

It was a shock, then, to discover that she had no intention of meeting me face-to-face. During the several months of revisions and proofing that preceded publication, I didn't lay eyes on her. We communicated via little notes that I left with and retrived from the receptionist. I never made it into the editorial sanctum.

Finally, tired of all this, I called to insist that we get together to plan some publicity. A meeting was set up but on the day appointed, I met only the firm's publicist. Jeanne Glass didn't even cross the hall to say hello. It was clear to me that though she might find my work admirable, she didn't care to shake my hand.

Nor did my problems end on publication day. I had given Pyramid a list of gay newspapers which, I knew, would review the novel. Six weeks after publication not one review copy had gone out. When I called Glass about this she was evasive. Finally I offered to do the mailing myself. At this I was told that no free copies would be given me — I would have to buy them at the usual author's discount. Nor would envelopes or postage be forthcoming — these would be at my expense too. I'm afraid that conversation ended in a shouting match; I never spoke to my editor at Pyramid again.

It is a testament to the perspicacity of gay people and the power of the gay grapevine that the book succeeded. Despite the fact that there was nothing on the cover or blurb to signal that the protagonist was homosexual and the book's milieu entirely gay, despite the fact that no review appeared outside the gay press and the book was advertised only once (in the *Advocate*, at my own expense), *The Butterscotch Prince* sold almost 25,000 copies. I received countless letters, several expressions of interest from filmmakers, an advance toward a screenplay and a great many invitations to submit new manuscripts elsewhere. The book was taught in gay literature courses at several colleges. The little novel which I had written as a lark ended up by making friends for me all over the world (it did especially well in England).

In spite of all this, Pyramid, within a relatively brief period, shredded the unsold copies and removed the book from their list. My agent told me that their salesmen found it embarrassing. Thus the novel which, with proper promoting, might have continued to find readers for many years, was quietly dumped.

I mention these sad and demeaning details because it is easy to forget that a decade ago mainstream publishers were not interested in actively promoting a gay book to the gay market. Such an activity was beneath their dignity — it would require them to acknowledge and participate in a culture, a world, that they scorned. Gay books had to be disguised, prettified, distorted. Once published, they had to be kept in a literary closet for fear of offending salesmen, booksellers, browsers. This was both cynical and hypocritical; naturally, it almost guaranteed that a book would fail. Only a few small presses, usually gay-owned, proudly proclaimed their wares — within the limits of their small budgets. It is only since 1978, and with the pioneering efforts of a handful of commercial publishers, that the trade has changed its policy toward gay books. In this, as in so many other areas of gay life, profit rather than justice was the chief motive for change.

It was, therefore, with a great deal of pleasure that I

accepted the offer from Alyson Publications to reissue the novel. I was glad it would have a second life. How many of us, after all, get to see our children reincarnated? The only question confronting me, as I sat down to re-read the novel — ten years, almost to the day, since I had put the first blank page in my typewriter — was whether to revise it. As I read, it was obvious that the basic situation was still relevant and believable and the central relationship — that of Cord to his murdered friend Ellison — posed a dilemma that was still important. At the same time, the social and sexual world which served as background to the book had changed drastically.

After a lengthy debate with myself and with friends as to whether the novel wouldn't be better left untouched as a period piece, I decided to update and contemporize as unobtrusively as possible. My purpose now, as then, was chiefly to entertain. I decided this purpose could be best achieved by altering the background to reflect our present condition. I hope that my former readers will not be disappointed by the changes and that new readers will be diverted by what they encounter for the first time

Richard Hall
New York City

May 1983

Other ALYSON books you'll enjoy
Don't miss our *free book* offer on the last page

DEATH TRICK
Richard Stevenson; $5.95

When a sensational gay murder hits the headlines in Albany, New York, the prime suspect turns out to be a young gay activist who has disappeared. His socially prominent parents call in Don Strachey, a private eye in the classic tradition — with a difference. Strachey is a low-key but cocky detective known for getting results when the police can't, and for his connections in his own community — the gay community.

CHINA HOUSE
by Vincent Lardo; $5.95

If you've been waiting for a good story for a stormy night, one you won't want to put down, here it is. This new novel has all the romance and intrigue you'd hope for in a gay gothic. The author (whose pen name Julian Mark will be familiar to many readers) has created a suspenseful story complete with a deserted New England mansion, a handsome young heir haunted by the death of his twin brother, and a father-son relationship that's closer than most.

COMING OUT RIGHT
A handbook for the gay male
by William Hanson and Wes Muchmore; $5.95

Most gay men remember their first trip to a gay bar. It's a frightening and difficult step, often representing the transition from a life of secrecy and isolation into a world of unknowns.

That step will be easier for men who have read *Coming Out Right*. Here, the many facets of gay life are spelled out for the newcomer: how to meet other gay people; what to expect at bars, baths and cruising spots; the unique problems faced by men coming out when they're under 18 or over 30.... in short, here in one book is information you would otherwise spend years learning the hard way.

THE SPARTAN
by Don Harrison; $5.95

Pantarkes' goal is to enter the Olympics and win the laurel crown. But at the age of 16, after accidentally killing the son of a high official, Pantarkes is forced to flee his home in Sparta. For two years his Olympic dreams are postponed as he is drafted into the Theban army to help fight against the invading Macedonians; then finds himself in the middle of a revolt against the Spartan tyrants who had earlier forced him to flee.

This brisk-paced novel provides a vivid picture of classical Greece and the early Olympics, and of an era when gay relationships were a common and valued part of life.

BETWEEN FRIENDS
by Gillian E. Hanscombe; $5.95

Frances and Meg were friends in school, years ago; now Frances is a married housewife while Meg is involved in lesbian politics. Through letters between the two women and some of their friends, *Between Friends* tells an engrossing story while exploring issues that apply to all of us: monogamy, communal living, relationships, racism, and parenthood.

FRANNY: THE QUEEN OF PROVINCETOWN
by John Preston; $3.95

Even if you dressed Franny in leather, he'd still look like a queen. It's the way he walks, his little mannerisms, and his utter unwillingness to change them or hide them that give him away.

And there's something else about Franny. It's a way he has of coming into your life and making his mark on it. As Franny's boys can tell you, once you know the Queen of Provincetown, your life may never be the same.

ONE TEENAGER IN TEN
edited by Ann Heron; $3.95

One teenager in ten is lesbian or gay. Here, 26 young people tell about how they came to discover their homosexuality; about how and whether they told their parents and friends; about what it's like to come out at an age when being different takes a special kind of courage.

$TUD
by Phil Andros; $6.95

In the 1960s, while other writers were churning out mass-produced, formula porn, Samuel Steward (under the penname Phil Andros) was different. He was a former English professor and a tattoo artist (trade name: Phil Sparrow); he also had a good sense of humor. All these qualities came together in the Phil Andros stories, which elevated gay erotic writing to a new level. Now we have re-issued *$tud* in a new edition, with an introduction by John Preston. If you remember *$tud* from the sixties you'll be glad to know it's back. If you didn't read it then, you're lucky. You can still read these stories for the first time.

THE ADVOCATE GUIDE TO GAY HEALTH
R.D. Fenwick; $6.95

You'd expect a good gay health book to cover a wide range of information, and this one does. What you wouldn't expect is that it could be so enjoyable to read! Here you'll find the expected information about sexually-transmitted diseases; you'll also learn about such things as what you should know before going into sex therapy; how some lesbians and gay men have handled their fear about aging; and the important lessons of the holistic health movement.

Get this book free!

When were you last outraged by prejudiced media coverage of gay people? Chances are it hasn't been long. *Talk Back!* tells how you, in surprisingly little time, can do something about it.

If you order at least three other books from us, you may request a FREE copy of this important book. (See order form on next page.)

Talk Back!

The Gay Person's Guide to Media Action

Lesbian and Gay Media Advocates

To get these books:

Ask at your favorite bookstore for the books listed here. You may also order by mail. Just fill out the coupon below, or use your own paper if you prefer not to cut up this book.

GET A FREE BOOK! When you order any three books listed here at the regular price, you may request a *free* copy of *Talk Back!*

BOOKSTORES: Standard trade terms apply. Details and catalog available on request.

— — — — — — — — — — — — — — — — — —

Enclosed is $_____ for the following books. (Add $1.00 postage when ordering just one book; if you order two or more, we'll pay the postage.)

☐ The Advocate Guide to Gay Health ($6.95)
☐ Between Friends ($5.95)
☐ Butterscotch Prince ($4.95)
☐ China House ($4.95)
☐ Coming Out Right ($5.95)
☐ Death Trick ($5.95)
☐ Franny: The Queen of Provincetown ($3.95)
☐ One Teenager in Ten ($3.95)
☐ Quatrefoil ($6.95)
  (*A re-issue of the classic 1950 gay novel*)
☐ Reflections of a Rock Lobster ($4.95)
  (*The true story of Aaron Fricke, who made national news when he took a male date to his high school prom.*)
☐ Spartan ($5.95)
☐ $tud ($6.95)
☐ Send a free copy of *Talk Back!* as offered above. I have ordered at least three other books.

name: _____

address: _____

city:_____state:_____zip:_____

ALYSON PUBLICATIONS
PO Box 2783, Dept. B-29, Boston, Mass. 02208

This offer expires December 31, 1984. After that date, please write for current catalog.